WITHDRAWN

The Case of the
Vampire Vacuum Sweeper

John R. Erickson

Illustrations by Gerald L. Holmes

Puffin Books

For Gary Rinker,

a good man to ride the river with.

PUFFIN BOOKS
Published by the Penguin Group
Penguin Putnam Books for Young Readers,
345 Hudson Street, New York, New York 10014, U.S.A.
Penguin Books Ltd,
27 Wrights Lane, London W8 5TZ, England
Penguin Books Australia Ltd,
Ringwood, Victoria, Australia
Penguin Books Canada Ltd,
10 Alcorn Avenue, Toronto, Ontario, Canada M4V 3B2
Penguin Books (N.Z.) Ltd,
182-190 Wairau Road, Auckland 10, New Zealand

Penguin Books Ltd, Registered Offices:
Harmondsworth, Middlesex, England

First published in the United States of America
by Maverick Books, Gulf Publishing Company, 1997
Published by Puffin Books, a member of
Penguin Putnam Books for Young Readers, 1999

7 9 10 8 6

ISBN 0-14-130405-7

Hank the Cowdog® is a registered trademark of John R. Erickson.

Printed in the United States of America

CONTENTS

Mysterious Esther Appears on the Ranch

It's me again, Hank the Cowdog. When I heard the noise, I knew we had serious problems. I'll admit that I didn't know the cause right away, and I never suspected that it might have been caused by an enemy agent named Mysterious Esther.

Nor did I have any suspicions that before the night was over, I would be attacked by a Vampire Vacuum Sweeper. All I knew was that we had us a wild stampede down at the weaning pen, and I had to stop it before the calves tore down the fence and scattered into four counties.

It was in November, as I recall, yes, because that's when we rounded up all the cattle, separated

1

the calves from their mothers, and weaned them. The calves, that is. We weaned the calves. We don't wean the mothers because they're already weaned.

We wean the calves off their mommas' milk, don't you see, because it's time for them to get out and hustle their own grub, like the rest of us. We put 'em together in a bunch and feed 'em alfalfa hay and store-bought feed for a couple of weeks. No problem there. The problem is that they are little dummies, afraid of every little noise and shadow, and once they start running, they'll flatten fences and scatter like quail.

It's called a stampede, and that's what we had cooking. I knew it just as soon as I heard the rumble of their hooves.

We were down at Slim's place, don't you see, on the front porch. We were, uh, guarding the porch and the woodpile. Or to be perfectly accurate about it and to call a spade a shovel, I was guarding the woodpile while my assistant was in the process of sleeping his life away.

I was standing guard, see. Why? Well, we'd gotten some secret information that there was a thief in the neighborhood, some nut who went creeping around ranches and stealing their woodpiles and porches.

It's true. Several whole entire porches had been

stolen, and I guess you know where I stand on the issue of porch-thieving. I don't allow it. By George, if a guy wants to steal a porch, he'd better go to the next ranch. If he tries it here, he has to deal with the Head of Ranch Security.

Anyways, that's what I was doing down at Slim's place, and when I heard the rumble of hooves, I came flying out of a deep . . . out of a deep state of, uh, concentration and thought about the problem of Porch Theft.

My ears sprang to the Alert Position. "Drover, the porkchops are cascading across the honking sassafras!"

Mister Nap-in-the-Afternoon leaped to his feet and began squeaking. "Who? Where are they? How many do you see?"

"They came out of the woodpile and they're trying to steal our porch."

He shook the vapors out of his head and stared at me. "Oh, hi Hank. Gosh, I must have been asleep and I dreamed that a honking porkchop was trying to steal our porch."

I raised up and blinked my eyes. There was Drover, giving me his usual empty stare. "What are you talking about?"

"Well . . . I'm not sure, but I think you said . . ."

"Never mind what I said. I was lost in thought,

Drover, deepest thought, and you interrupted my deepest porkchops with your . . ." Suddenly, I heard the rumble of hooves down at the weaning trap. "Holy smokes, Drover, the calves are running. We've got to warn Slim. Where is he?"

"Well, let's see here. Before we went to sleep, I saw him walking down to the hay barn."

"Hmmm, yes. Hay, barn, walking. It all fits the pattern. Go on."

"Well, he said he was going down there to see Esther."

I stared into his eyes. He had two of them. "See Esther? Who's Esther? Out with it, Drover, we haven't a moment to spare."

"Well, I'm not sure. But that's what he said, that he was going to the hay barn to see Esther."

"Hmmm, very strange. Okay, pardner, stand by for a rapid sprint to the hay barn. We've got to warn Slim about the stampede. Come on, let's go."

And with that, we went to Full Flames on all engines and went streaking to the hay barn—which, by the way, wasn't much of a barn. It was a small shed, made of weathered lumber and with a tin roof on the . . . well, on the top, of course. That's where you'd expect to find a roof, right? I notice these tiny details.

I was the first to arrive. Drover limped and lolly

4

gagged behind me, and I had to wait for him. This gave me a few precious moments to analyze the situation. It was clear by this time that the mysterious Esther had somehow spooked our cattle and caused them to stampede. At this point we didn't know how or why, but I was pretty sure that she was our prime suspect in the case. And Slim had to be warned.

At last Drover arrived, huffing and puffing. I greeted him with stern eyes. "Well, I'm glad you could join us, Drover. I hope this isn't interfering with your social schedule. Now listen carefully. We're going in. I'll go first, you cover the rear."

"Whose rear, mine or yours?"

"*Our rear*, Drover. We have only one rear."

"No, we've got two and mine's the one with the stub tail, and it's the one I sit on all the time."

I glared at the runt. "Are you trying to be funny?"

"I don't think so."

"Good. You're not. When I say 'our rear,' I mean our collective rear, the area behind us."

"Yeah, but what if we're facing the other direction?"

"Everything changes, Drover. In the blink of an eye, the front can become the rear and the rear can become the front. We have to be prepared for any contagency."

"Oh, okay. So we're not supposed to blink our eyes?"

I heaved a deep sigh. Sometimes, when I talk to Drover . . . oh well. We had work to do. "Never mind. We're going in, and you'd better cover the rear."

"Well, all right, but I still don't understand . . ."

I didn't wait around to hear the rest. I crept up to the door, peered inside (it was dark), and then went charging in, barking in all directions. I was a little surprised that Mysterious Esther was nowhere in sight. I was even more surprised—shocked, actually—when I saw Slim sprawled out on a layer of hay.

"Cover the door, Drover. We've got a man down."

"Yeah, I guess he took a nap."

"Are you nuts? He's *unconscious*. Mysterious Esther is obviously a spy. She clubbed Slim from behind and now she's out there stampeding our cattle. Don't you see how it all fits together?"

"Not really, and you know what else?"

"Is this important, Drover? We've got a man down and an enemy spy running loose on the ranch. This isn't a great time to be making small talk."

"Yeah, but I just figured it out."

I studied him with narrowed eyes. "You figured it out? Drover, you don't need to figure it out because I figured it out long ago. Don't forget who's in charge here."

He gave me a silly grin. "Yeah, but I just figured out what Slim said. He didn't say he was going to 'see Esther.' He said he was going to take a 'siesta,' only he called it a 'see-ester,' and that's why he's asleep. Pretty neat, huh?"

I held him in my glare for a long, throbbing moment. "Drover, that's the dumbest thing you've said in weeks. In the first place, we've already put out a tracer on Mysterious Esther, and we know she's a spy. In the second place, your phony explanation doesn't account for the stampede that is occurring at this very moment. I'm sorry, Drover, but your can of worms just doesn't cut bait."

At that very moment, just as I had disposed of Drover's ridiculous theory, I heard a noise behind me. In one rapid motion, I whirled around and cut loose with a withering barrage of . . . hmm, Slim seemed to be coming out of his coma, the one brought on by a savage blow to his head.

That was good news, great news. By George, I'd been pretty worried about him. I cancelled all barks and leaped up on the hay beside his potsrate body and began giving him Emergency CPR Licks on the face. That brought him around.

He pushed me away and said, "Quit." Then he

sat up and yawned. "You birdbrains. I come down to the hay barn to take me a little nap and you show up like ants at a church picnic, barkin' your fool heads off. You got something against hired hands takin' a little see-ester?"

HUH?

I cut my eyes from side to side. Okay, maybe Drover had . . .

If he was going to take a nap, why didn't he just call it a nap? How can a dog run a ranch when people go around speaking in five different languages?

Siesta baloney.

Suddenly Slim cocked his ear and listened. "Good honk, dogs, the calves are running!" He grabbed his hat and headed for the corrals. For a moment Drover and I were alone. I beamed him a glare of purest steel. He gave me his usual silly grin.

"Drover, sometimes I think you're trying to make a mockery of my position on this ranch."

"Yeah, but I figured it out, didn't I?"

"Even a blind hog finds a piece of baloney once in a while."

"What does that mean?"

I didn't have time to explain the obvious. I went streaking down to the corrals, where we found . . . you'd be shocked if I told you we found Mysterious Esther, wouldn't you? Well, we didn't, and for the very best of reasons. Obviously, she didn't exist. She'd come straight out of the trash heap of Drover's imagination.

No, we didn't find Mysterious Esther. We found Slim standing beside the fence, watching 146 head of insane steers and heifers running around the weaning pen. I took up a position right beside him, and together we beamed disgusted looks at the cattle.

"Stupid calves, what's got into 'em now? Uh-oh. Do you see what I'm a-seein'? Stray dogs, Hank, four of 'em, and they're chasing our little darlings. I'll go for my shotgun. You go whup the tar out of 'em."

Yes sir!

And so the adventure began.

CHAPTER TWO

I Arrest
Four Stray Dogs

Slim trotted off to the house. I whirled around and was ready to address Drover when he came limping up. "Okay, men, here's the situation. We've got a Code Three out there in the weaning pen. It's liable to be a combat engagement, so lock and load, and prepare for the worst. Any questions?"

Drover raised his paw. "Yeah, this old leg's about to quit me."

"That's not a question, trooper. We'll handle complaints after the battle. Any more questions?"

Drover raised his paw. "Can I go home?"

"Negative. You'll join me in combat against four stray dogs."

His eyes popped open. "Four stray dogs! I thought it was a woman spy. Boy, I sure get confused."

"You're right, Drover, but being right for once won't get you out of combat. And neither will being confused. Let's hit the beach and give 'em the full load of barking. Good luck, men."

And with that, we shot under the fence and went streaking out into the weaning pen. I could see them now, four scruffy-looking mutts who'd drifted out from town and were shopping around for trouble. Well, they'd come to the right place for that.

As I drew closer and got a better look at the mutts, I realized that I'd seen them before. It was Buster and Muggs and their gang of town dogs. Remember them? I absorbed this information with . . . uh . . . mixed emotions, shall we say. On the one hand, I knew they were double-tough. On the other hand, heh heh, I knew that Slim's shotgun was even double-tougher.

A guy doesn't worry much about the opposition when he's bucked up by backshot. Backed up by buckshot, I should say, and sometimes it even makes him a little . . . well, cocky, you might say. Confident. Braver than normal. Secure in his feelings of self-esteem.

I headed straight for them and switched on all flashing lights and sirens. Oh, and I also yelled, "Pull over, you creeps, I want to have a word with you! And be quick about it."

When they ignored my warnings, I had no choice but to crash into the one in the lead—Buster, as it turned out, the leader of the gang. Boy, you should have seen him . . . actually, the crashing-into deal had a worse effect on me than on him. He was stouter than you might have thought, is the point, and maybe I was the one who got rolled.

But he stopped, and so did his boys, and that was the whole point of the exercise, right? Sure it was. I got 'em shut down. I picked myself up and marched over to them. A glance toward the house told me that Slim was already out on the porch, loading shells into his pump shotgun. That gave me fresh reserves of courage.

When I marched up to them, Buster was talking to his pals. "Say, what was that thing I just ran into? Was it a fly or a gnat?"

Muggs, who had the build of a bulldog and the brain of a fencepost, was bouncing up and down on his short, thick legs. "Nah, it was the jerk, Boss, right there, see him? He ran into you and I saw it, I saw the whole thing."

Buster looked me up and down. "Oh yeah, I think you're right, Muggsie. Say, jerk, when you're out running and playing, you need to be more careful. You could get yourself hoit, running into objects made of steel and iron."

12

Muggs stuck his nose in my face. "Yeah, jerk, and if the boss don't steal your object, I just might have to iron your face, har har. Did you hear that one, Boss? Huh? Wasn't that pretty good, huh?"

"That was very clever, Muggsie. I find myself astonished, as you might say." Buster's gaze drifted over to me. "So what kind of foolish impulse brings you into our midst?"

I cleared my throat. "Okay, this won't take long."

Muggsie was back in my face. "It better not, jerk, 'cause the longer it takes, the shorter you'll be."

I pushed his face away. "Would you point that hot air somewhere else? Thanks. Maybe you can kill a few weeds."

Buster grinned. "Say, that ain't bad. Did you hear that, boys? Muggsie might kill some weeds with his breath." The others laughed. Buster's gaze remained on me. "Go on, hero, I can hardly wait to hear your message. Let me guess. You ain't fond of us chasing your cows, correct?"

"That's right, only they're not cows, Buster. Cows are adult animals. You're chasing steers and heifers, but I guess that's a little too complicated for you guys."

His eyes grew wide. "Ooooo! Hey boys, we thought we was chasing cows, but they ain't cows. They're heffs and steroids." They all laughed. "So what's the point, country boy? Somehow, your cows just started runnin' and we couldn't figger out why, could we, boys?" That got a laugh. "So was we doing something bad? 'Cause if we were, me and my boys might feel terrible about it."

"Chasing cattle is against Ranch Law, Buster. You know that as well as I do."

"I do? Then you tink we was doing it just for meanness?" He rolled his eyes toward the sky. "I fear my heart will break."

Muggsie jumped back into the conversation. "Yeah, jerk, and then I fear we'll have to broke your face, and after we broke your face, we'll broke your nose off too, won't we, Boss?"

"Shat up, Muggs. I appreciate your interest, but let 'im talk."

"Thanks. You have two minutes to get off my ranch."

"Wow. Two minutes. That ain't much time, and me and the boys was having fun and maybe we can't make it, see? So I wonder what might happen."

I gave them an easy smile. "You guys ever go up against a shotgun?"

"Yeah. Lots of times. It ain't fun. But you know what?" He drilled me in the chest with his paw. "You ain't got one, jerk. That could be a problem— I mean, with you mouthing off and everything."

Muggs was back. "Yeah, jerk, and if you don't mouth stopping off, I'm gonna . . . if you don't get that shotgun outa your mouth . . . if you don't . . ."

Buster stopped him with a raised paw. "Tink about it, Muggsie. It'll come to you in a minute." Back to me. "Me and my boys obsoive that you ain't got a shotgun, pal."

I swallowed hard. What the heck was Slim doing! "It's . . . it's up on the porch, Buster, and it'll be here any minute now. That's Slim and he's doubling all the charges."

"Is he? But the problem is that he ain't here, and you are, and he ain't mouthing off to me and my boys—and you are. Do you see what this means?"

I laughed in their faces. "Ha, ha. Buster, you don't really think I'd be stupid enough to walk into the middle of you guys without a secret weapon, do you?"

He thought about that. "Yeah, I do. I honestly do. I tink you're that dumb, and I thought so the minute I laid eyes on you. Somehow you just look . . . dumb."

"What if I told you that I've got a whole division of Rottweilers hiding in those chinaberry trees, just waiting for my signal to attack?"

He shrugged. "Well, naturally I'd tink you was lying."

"Ha, ha, ha! Okay, guys, it's time for me to reveal that you've walked right into my trap."

Buster grinned. "Oh gosh, we have walked into his trap. What shall we do?"

Muggsie popped up. "Hey Boss, we could always run."

"Uh-uh. We ain't gonna run 'cause he ain't got a trap. He's all mouth and no brains, Muggsie, and in that respect he reminds me of . . . you."

I stiffened my back and tried to hide the quiver in my voice. "I'll give you to the count of three. At that point, we'll find out who's bluffing."

Buster nodded his head. "Yeah, we will, only I already know."

"ONE!"

Zoom! I went to Full Flames on all engines and made a wild dash for the house.

Sure, I knew it wasn't dignified for the Head of Ranch Security to be chased up on his own porch, but at that moment I didn't much care about appearances and so forth.

You'll be proud to know that I made it. I flew up on the porch, skidded to a stop, and took refuge . . . that is, I established a new command post behind . . . okay, I hid behind Slim's legs, but the important thing is that I began firing off barks immediately, and I mean big barks, huge barks,

barks that would have scared the liver out of a liverwurst sandwich.

Boy, you should have seen me. First I fired off two barks around Slim's left leg, then shifted sides (to confuse them, don't you know) and fired off two more barks around his right leg. Pretty impressive, huh? You bet it was.

And then—this will impress you even more— I poked my head *between his legs* and showered those hoodlums with a burst of Fully Automatic

Barking. It stopped 'em in their tracks, I mean, those guys were so shocked and terrified, they turned and ran like the cowards they really were.

Okay, maybe it helped that Slim finally got his shotgun loaded and sent a full chorus of buckshot singing over their heads, but mainly it was my Counter Offensive of deep, manly barking that turned the tide of battle in our favor. As the cowards vanished into the distance, I crept out of my Bunker Position and went charging after them. I went all the way to the edge of the porch, if you can believe that.

"Let that be a lesson to you, you meanies! And don't forget that your mommas are twice as ugly as you are!"

Boy, I got 'em told, huh? You bet I did. I had a feeling we'd never see those guys again. After I'd sent the rascals fleeing for their lives, I turned a sour gaze on Slim.

He grinned and shrugged. "Derned gun jammed on me."

Great. Swell. But wasn't there a new miracle invention called *gun oil*? I mean, some guys actually oiled their shotguns once or twice a year, and guess what—their shotguns didn't jam! And their dogs didn't get chased up on porches either.

Oh well, we'd won a huge moral victory over

the stray dogs and I had saved the calves from being stampeded all over the county, and maybe I could find it in my heart to forgive Slim for being . . . whatever he was. Lazy, I guess, and just a little careless with his Head of Ranch Security.

Perhaps you're wondering what became of Drover in all the excitement. I wondered about that myself, and it took me half an hour to solve the mystery. Actually, it was no mystery at all. It was the biggest non-surprise of the year. In the heat of battle, he had run back to the hay barn and had squeezed himself in between two bales of hay.

I discovered his hiney sticking out. We needn't report the full extent of the tongue-lashing I gave him. It was pretty severe, but he promised never to do it again, and this time, I got the feeling that he really meant it.

And with that, we retired to the house—and yes, to the warmth and comfort of Slim's wood-burning stove.

CHAPTER THREE

A Phone Call
in the Night

L et me say right here that I don't totally approve
of ranch dogs sleeping inside a house. Have I
mentioned that before? Maybe not, but it's true. Too
much warmth and comfort can corrupt a ranch dog.

I don't worry about myself, but I worry a lot
about Drover. I've noticed that he is easily corrupted
by luxuries, such as sleeping inside Slim's house.

Okay, maybe I sort of enjoy it too, but at least
I feel guilty about it. Show me a dog who feels no
guilt about sleeping inside a house and I'll show you
a dog who's on the roan to ruid.

Road to ruin, I should say. I'll show you a dog
who is being slowly strangled by the velvet glove
of luxury. It's a terrible thing to see.

Drover curled up on a spot near the stove and

20

within seconds he was totally knocked out—sleeping and making his usual orchestra of weird sounds, such as wheezing and grunting. Me, I couldn't sleep. Not only was I being distracted by Drover's noises, but I also began to notice that the floor was getting hard. I moved around and tried to find a comfortable spot, but nothing seemed to help. At last I heaved a weary sigh, jacked myself off the floor, and began a routine which we call Digging and Fluffing.

See, a lot of times when your bed's too hard, you can work it around and soften it up. First, we dig up the sleeping area with our front paws, then, second, we circle the softened spot three or four times before collapsing.

Anyways, I began the Digging and Fluffing Routine, and I knew right away that this was not going to be an easy assignment. Slim's hardwood floors were covered with carpet, but it was old and thin. I dug and dug and dug. Slim must have heard the sound of my claws scraping across his so-called carpet, because his eyes came up from the livestock paper he was reading.

"Hank, if I'd wanted a basement in this house, I would have dug it myself."

I stopped digging and stared at him. *Basement.* I wasn't digging a basement, I was merely trying to find a small comfortable spot on his . . . oh, maybe he was trying to be funny. Cowboy humor. They say one thing and mean something else.

Okay, digging a basement. Very funny.

I went back to my digging. He reached out his bare foot and kicked me on the tail section. Kind of gave me a jolt. I mean, I was in very deep concentration and . . .

"Quit tearing up my carpet. I paid fourteen dollars for that thing at a garage sale, and I don't need you digging holes in it. It ain't much, but it's better than you deserve."

Okay. Fine. If that's the way he felt about it, I would just . . . I didn't know what I was going to do. Sit up all night. Suffer. Deprive myself of much-needed sleep.

Just then, the silence was slashed by a loud piercing sound. I didn't know what it was, but I leaped away from it and began barking. At first, it sounded like . . . well, the ringing of some kind of bell or buzzer, perhaps an Early Warning Alarm, and when we dogs get an Early Warning Alarm, our first and most important response is to bark.

I barked, and since I wasn't sure where the sound was coming from, I delivered several bursts of Spray Barking and covered the entire north half of the . . .

Okay, relax. It was just the ringing of the tele-phone. Slim answered it.

"Hello. Yes. Not yet. It ain't nine o'clock. Uh-huh. Readin' my livestock paper and baby-sittin' a couple of souphounds. Who is this?" Suddenly, he sat up straight and his eyes popped open. "Viola? I'll be derned. How have you been? Haven't seen you in quite a spell. How's the grass down your way? Uh-huh. Same here. Cows are doing good."

I waited to hear something important. I mean, I'm a fairly busy dog and I usually have more important things to do than listen to Slim's Grass Report. My mind began to wander, is the point, and I found myself thinking of other matters.

I noticed, for example, the pile of newspapers on the floor near Slim's bare feet, and it occurred to me that those papers would make good bedding if a guy just took the time to work them around. I advanced toward the papers and shifted into Digging and Fluffing.

Now this was more like it! Instead of digging into a threadbare carpet, I had something with body and soul and substance. I dug and I dug, and you know, it was kind of satisfying, stirring up all those newspapers. Here was something worth digging, and I could hardly wait to shift into the next two steps in the procedure: Fluff and Circle the Bed.

I threw myself into the digging. By George, this was fun! It had been months since I had dug into a pile of newspapers this deep. I had 'em flying in all directions and was about ready to shift into the Fluffing Procedure, when I felt Slim's foot poke me in the ribs.

He covered the phone with his hand and gave me a hard glare. "Quit diggin' up my library, you dingbat. I have them papers filed just the way I want 'em and I may want to go back and clip out some articles. You're making a mess of my house."

I stared at him in disbelief. I was . . . ho boy, that was the joke of the century! Me making a mess of his house! Ha. His house was a slum area, and I'd had nothing to do with it.

He went back to his conversation. "Huh? No, I was talking to Hank. I think he wants to be a badger when he grows up. He's been trying to dig up my house all evening."

Well, there was another insult. For his information, I did *not* want to be a badger, I was perfectly content being a dog, thank you, but finding a comfortable place to relax in his house just happened to be no can of wax.

Okay, I stopped digging in his so-called library and moved rapidly into the Fluffing Procedure. With a little luck, I might have a decent place to sleep before midnight. I did some fluffing, then went right into Circle the Bed. I circled it three times, just the way it's supposed to be done, and then I plopped . . .

Yee-ow!

For Pete's sake, what was that thing I'd plopped down on? It felt like a rock, maybe even a boulder, and what was a boulder doing in the middle of Slim's living room? I raised myself to a standing position and began sniffing through the pile of papers, and even went to the trouble of activating Smelloradar.

A lot of dogs wouldn't have gone to that much trouble, but I did, for the simple reason that I wasn't too keen on the idea of sleeping on a rock pile.

Yes, I did have hopes of getting a little sleep, if I could clear away all the rubble and get Slim off the phone.

I had a boulder lurking in my bed and I had to find it. I activated Smelloradar and set it for Rock Search. Nothing, a total blank for rocks and boulders. But then . . . hmmm, I began picking up faint signals that suggested the presence of . . . bone?

Impossible. I punched in Deep Sniff and did a more thorough analysis. By George, all the instruments kept bringing up the same results: *Bone,*

grade three, fairly old, possibly steak. Well, a guy has to trust his instruments, so I probed deeper into the paper mess with my nose, and . . .

I'll be derned. Found a bone at the bottom of the heap.

My first thought was that some stranger had wandered into Slim's shack, gotten lost in all the papers and mess, and perished, leaving a few bones behind. But no, on second thought, that theory didn't make sense. Nobody in his right mind would wander into Slim's dirty house.

But what was a bone doing in the middle of the living room?

I eased my jaws around the bone, lifted it out of the paper mess, laid it on the floor, and studied it with eyes that were well trained in the field of Bonology. The results were shocking. Not only was this not a steak bone, it wasn't even a beef bone. It was a *turkey neck bone*!

What was a turkey neck bone doing in the middle of Slim's living room floor? I had no idea. All I can tell you is that many strange things end up on his floor.

Well, I felt pretty proud of myself for solving the Mystery of the Turkey Neck Bone, and it occurred to me that maybe I should celebrate my success by chewing it. That's just what I did.

I had just taken it into my mouth and begun to enjoy the nice crunchy texture of this particular bone, and had lost all interest in Slim's phone conversation with Miss Viola when, suddenly, he hung up the phone and leaped to his feet.

I stared at him in shock and surprise. I mean, Slim wasn't much inclined to making sudden movements of any kind. Leaping out of a chair was something you might expect him to do if the house was on fire and burning boards were falling all around him, but here and now?

I noticed that his eyes were wide with . . . something. Fear. Terror. Something bad had happened. Something was terribly wrong. The bone rolled out of my mouth and I went straight into Heavy-Duty Barking.

"Good honk," he yelled over the sound of my barking, "Viola's folks are out of coffee. She's coming over here to borrow some. She'll be here in thirty minutes and this house looks like a train wreck. And Hank, shut up your barking!"

HUH?

Shut up my . . . okay, sure, fine. I could shut up my barking. I'd just been trying . . . I mean, he'd been the one who'd flowed out of the chair, right? Floed. Flewed. Flowned.

Leaped. He'd been the one who had leaped out of his chair, right? When people start leaping out of chairs and windows, screeching and rolling their eyes, we dogs are trained to bark. But if he didn't want his house to be protected and alerted by a highly trained, highly decorated Head of Ranch Security, that was just fine with me.

I had better things to do than bark, such as crunching that turkey neck bone.

Now, where was that bone? I poked my nose into the piles of paper and was in the process of . . .

"Out of the way, dogs, we've got to get this place cleaned up!"

Here he came, lumbering and thundering right over the top of me. Fortunately, I saw him coming and was able to scramble out of the way. His big bare foot missed smashing my nose by a matter of inches. Too bad his big bare foot didn't miss the bone.

Let's get something straight right here. I refuse to take responsibility for what happened next. Remember, I was just minding my own business. Remember also that the bone had been in that same room, on that same floor, in that same mess of papers for months.

Okay, maybe my chewing had sharpened some of the ends and edges, but don't forget that turkey neck bones, even those that haven't been chewed, are pretty jagged, nothing you'd want to pounce on with a bare foot.

That's what he did. He pounced on the bone, the jagged, sharp turkey vertebra, with his bare foot, and that began a very strange chain of events.

CHAPTER FOUR

Attacked by— Something Awful...

As near as I can figure, he stepped on the bone pretty hard, which probably hurt. Of course it did, which explains his howl of pain. But that wasn't the worst part. He also twisted his ankle and went crashing to the floor.

The crash brought Drover out of his stuporous state. He leaped to his feet, staggered around, and began squeaking. "Help, murder, mayday! The porkchops are coming! Oh my leg!"

In a flash, he was gone. I heard his claws scratching on the floor as he crawled beneath the bed in the back room.

Slim grabbed his ankle (his own ankle, not Drover's) and let out a groan. I rushed to his side and began administering Emergency Licks to his face and ear—for the second time that evening, I might add. I mean, this was clearly a serious situation, him falling to the floor, and I was willing to forget his hateful remarks about my barking and put the past behind us.

Do you suppose he was grateful? Oh no. He turned to me with wild eyes and clenched teeth and screeched, *"Get away from me, you meathead, I think I've broke my ankle!"*

Fine. By George, if he thought he could cure his broken ankle without Emergency Licks, that was sure okay with me.

I was just trying to help.

Sometimes I wonder what it takes to please these people.

I retired to the northeast corner of the room, sat down, and began beaming him Hurtful Looks and Brooding Glares.

He clenched his teeth against the pain and struggled to his feet, using a chair for support. He tested the ankle several times before putting his weight on it, and that brought another grimace of pain. Then he tried walking on it—or hopping might be a better word for it, because he sure was packing it around. But he managed to walk a few steps before he hoisted 'er up and stopped for a rest.

"Well, I don't think she's busted. I hope not, 'cause a broke leg don't fit into my plans right now."

Was he talking to me? Too bad, because I wasn't listening. I no longer cared, and to prove it, I turned my eyes away from him.

I mean, we dogs are very sensitive animals. We can be screeched at and yelled at so many times, and then something terrible happens to our . . . whatever.

He limped a few more steps. "I guess it'll be all right. I wonder what that thing was that I stepped on."

My ears jumped. My gaze slid over in his direction. Stepped on? Had he stepped on something? I, uh, had no idea what it might have been. Probably some irregularity in the, uh, floorboarding. The floor was pretty old.

He hopped and limped over to the scene of the accident and peered down into the jumble of papers and so forth. His brows jumped. Uh-oh. He reached down with his hand and came up holding the . . . uh . . . that is, holding some sort of white, irregular-shaped object, perhaps a bone. He turned it around in his fingers, then I felt his gaze moving across the room and . . . well, searching for me, perhaps, although . . .

His eyes locked on me. I found it hard to meet

32

his gaze, so to speak, and began studying the holes, nails, and paint splatters on the north wall.

"Hank." I jumped at the sound of his voice. "What is this?"

I turned my eyes in his direction. I was feeling very uncomfortable about this. He was holding something in his fingers, it appeared.

"What is this?"

I, uh, thumped my tail on the floor and squeezed up my most sincere smile.

His eyes came at me like drill bits. I could feel them drilling holes in me. "Where'd this turkey bone come from?"

Turkey bone? Oh yes, the, uh, thing in his fingers. Well, turkey bones came from . . . turkeys, so to speak, and maybe a lost turkey had wandered into the house and . . . couldn't find its way out and just died.

Yes, that was it. The turkey had died in the house and . . . its bones had gotten scattered to the four winds, as they say, and one of the neck bones had . . . well, suddenly turned up on the, uh, living room floor.

But the important point was that it had been pretty muchly a natural occurrence and we dogs knew nothing about it, almost nothing at all. No kidding.

I swept my tail across the threadbare carpet floor and concentrated extra hard on putting sincerity into my, uh, expression.

"You bozo. You were chewing a turkey bone in my living room, weren't you?"

Well, I . . .

"And I stepped on it and almost broke my leg."

Well, you see . . . oh boy. All at once I felt that the facts had overwhelmed my ability to explain them. I switched over to Slow Mournful Wags on the tail section and gave him my most sincere look of tragedy.

Okay. Yes. The cat was out of the sandbag. I could no longer deny the awful truth. I stood before him, accused and convicted of terrible crimes, and now all that was left for me was to throw myself at his feet and hope for mercy.

I lowered my head and assumed the pose of a beaten dog, a humbled dog; a dog who had fallen to the very depths of despair and heartbreak; who had hoped and wanted all his life to be a good dog, but who was now feeling the terrible stinging lash of conscience.

I lowered myself to the very depths of the floor and crawled, yes, crawled, to his towering, angry presence. And licked his big toe.

Sometimes that works, you know.

He continued to glare down at me, but I noticed a few cracks in his icy expression. Maybe it was working. I rolled my eyes up to him and wiggled the very tip end of my tail. Yes, the ice was melting. The stone was showing a few cracks.

He shook his head and compressed his lips. "Hank, you're such a birdbrain. You're just dumb. Do you know that?"

Well, I . . . I wasn't in a position to, uh, argue that.

"You're dumb and you're pretty close to worthless, and I could have broke my neck, as well as my leg, on your dadgum turkey bone." He sighed and glanced around the room. "But I didn't, so I guess I'll start cleaning up this . . . good honk, this place looks awful!"

There it was. I was saved, oh happy day! I went to Joyous Bounds and Leaps, wrapped my front paws around his leg, and gave him a big hug.

He reached down and scratched me behind the ears. "I get myself into the derndest messes, and I don't know whether it's because I'm too nice or too dumb. Probably dumb. I remember now how that turkey bone got in here. I bought that ten-pound package of turkey necks on sale and ate boiled necks for two weeks, and I was chewing on a bone one night and forgot to throw it in the trash. Sorry, Hankie. I got what I deserved. You're cleared of all charges."

See? Didn't I tell you? But the important thing was that we were friends again. Now all we had to do was get his house shaped up.

At first he just wandered from room to room like a lost child, muttering and shaking his head. Like a good, loyal dog, I followed him every step of the way. If I couldn't actually help him with the cleaning, at least I could be with him in his hour of greatest need and show him, through wags and solemn expressions, that I shared his pain and felt his sorrow.

This Sharing of Pain has always been a very important part of a cowdog's job. Even dogs who do poorly in other departments can keep their jobs by scoring well in the Sharing of Pain.

"Where do I start, with a match and a can of gasoline? Why did I answer that phone!"

He took a big gulp of air and plunged into the work. He attacked the newspapers first, scooping them up with both hands and stuffing them into grocery sacks. After he'd filled five sacks, we began to see that there was a floor and a carpet on the next level.

Well, that was progress. The job didn't seem as hopeless as it had before. Slim's mood began to improve and the dark shadows that had covered his face went away. Before long, he was even whistling.

At that point, we could see the entire floor of the living room, which was quite an accomplishment. The only problem was that the floor and the carpet needed to be swept. Even I could see that. I mean, we're talking about sand, gravel, dirt, pieces of grass and hay, and even a few muddy tracks that might have been there for years.

Slim got his broom and made a few swipes with it, but his heart wasn't in it. Then his eyes brightened. "Say, I've got an old vacuum sweeper in the hall closet. Sally May gave it to me a year ago and I forgot all about it. Stand by for action, Hankie, I'm going for the sweeper."

He ran for the sweeper, dragged it out, and plugged it in. All at once, the house was filled with the sounds of its screaming motor.

Slim yelled, "Kinda noisy, ain't it?"

Yes, it certainly was, and it hurt my ears so much that I found it necessary to turn my back on the awful thing. That was a mistake. I should have known better. Never turn your back on a cowboy who's armed with a vacuum sweeper.

You know what he did? I was shocked. I mean, there we were in the midst of an Emergency Cleanup, right? Miss Viola was due to arrive in twenty minutes and Slim didn't want her to see what a filthy pit he lived in, right? In other words, even if we worked like demons and never looked up, we had our hands cut out for us, right?

So what did Slim do? You won't believe this.

See, I was just sitting there, looking the other direction, minding my own business, trying to ignore the whining scream of the sweeper, when all of a sudden ...

YIKES!

Some mysterious something got hold of my tail and began . . .

It was a very strange sensation, and I mean very strange. It didn't exactly hurt but it scared the bejeebers out of me. I mean, all at once I felt that my tail was being pulled by some kind of wind or magnetic force into a . . . I don't know, into a black hole or a whirlpool.

WHHHHEEEEE

Well, you know me. When confronted with something strange and terrifying, I don't just sit there. I bark. Yes sir, I barked and whirled and leaped into the air and . . .

And looked straight into Slim's grinning face. I mean, he was grinning like some kind of devil monster, a childish devil monster, and would you care to guess what he was grinning about?

I should have known he couldn't stick with a job for more than thirty seconds, that his idle childish cowboy mind . . .

Just skip it. I'm not going to tell you the rest of it.

CHAPTER FIVE

Okay, Maybe It Was the Vacuum Sweeper

We've discussed cowboys and their pranks, right? Give them a simple job of work and before you know it, they're goofing off and thinking of jokes to pull on helpless bystanders—such as their loyal dogs.

Okay, I was sitting there in the middle of the living room, minding my own business and the next thing I knew, Slim was coming after me with the vacuum sweeper. Can you believe a grown man would do such a thing? I couldn't. But he sure did, and before I caught on to his foolish, childish, infantile foolishness, he had managed to suck most of my tail into the sweeper pipe.

What did I do? I ran, of course. I snatched my tail out of the Bottomless Sweeper Pipe, tucked it between my legs (my tail, that is), and made a dash for the nearest corner, where I sat down on my tail—just to make sure he couldn't get it again.

Oh, and I also beamed him Looks of Wounded Pride and Complete Astonishment.

Did that help? Did he take the hint that I didn't enjoy this? Oh no! Here he came again, grinning like a . . . I don't know what. Like a vampire, a crazed vampire who ate dog tails, and of course he had that screaming hissing sweeper pipe out in front of him, and in spite of all my hints and facial messages that *this wasn't funny*, he went after my tail again.

That did it. A dog can only take so much. I scrambled out of the corner, ducked under the coffee table, scrambled out the other side, and made a dash down the hall. Would you believe it? He followed me! I mean, he ran down that hall, limping on his bad foot and dragging the sweeper behind him and

attacking my tail section with the hissing pipe!

I was shocked. Astonished. Outraged. Who did this guy think he was and what kind of zoo was he running? Didn't he realize that it's very undignified for Heads of Ranch Security to flee from vacuum sweepers and take refuge under beds?

And what about cleaning the house? Just moments before, he had been in a panic that Miss Viola would see that he lived in a junkyard and know the awful truth—that he was nothing but a dirty bachelor whose habits would shame a hog.

It's impossible to explain the behavior of abnormal people and cowboys, and I gave up trying. I scrambled under the bed and found myself looking into Drover's moon-shaped eyes.

"Hi, Hank. Did you hear a funny sound?"

"I heard a sound, Drover, but it wasn't funny. I don't want to alarm you, but there's a crazy man out there, and he's armed with a tail-eating vacuum sweeper."

"Oh my gosh, I don't have much tail left!"

"Well, you'd better hang on to it, pal, because..."

My words were buried under the scream and hiss of the Vampire Vacuum Sweeper, as the dreaded hissing pipe invaded our sanctuary and began searching for our tails. Drover screeched. So did I, and we both banged our heads against the bottom of the bed as we scrambled to save our tails from that awful hissing Thing.

Do you know what saved us? Slim ran out of cord and jerked the plug out of the wall. Otherwise . . . there's no telling what might have happened. We might have been sucked into some terrible black hole or we might have lost our tails or we might have . . . I don't even want to think about it.

But the important thing is that our courageous behavior and stern barking caused the plug to pop out of the socket, and our lives and tails were saved just in the nickering of time. The scream of the motor and the hiss of the pipe died away. An eerie silence moved over us.

I glanced at Drover. "How you doing, pal?"

"Terrible. I can't feel my left front leg. I think it's cut off."

"Holy smokes, do you see any blood?"

"Well . . . I see dirt and lint and three dirty socks."

"I know, but blood, do you see any blood? If your leg had been torn off, you would notice some blood."

"How much?"

"I'm not sure. A quart, a gallon?"

"I don't see that much."

"Okay, how about a pint?"

"Nope."

"All right, how about a cup?"

There was a moment of silence. Then "Oh my gosh, Hank, there's a cup!"

"This is worse than I thought, Drover. It appears that you've been maimed by the Vampire Vacuum Sweeper. Your life will never be the same again."

"Yeah, and it was never the same to start with."

"What?"

"Every day's always been different. Now it'll be even worse."

"Hmmm, yes, of course. You'll have to make many adjustments, Drover. Life without a leg is legless in many ways."

"Oh my gosh, I won't be able to limp any more!"

"That's true. You know the old saying: A three-legged dog never limps."

"I've never heard that one."

"Actually, I just made it up, but it's true. Think about it, Drover. How could a three-dogged leg limp? I think it's impossible."

"Yeah, and any leg that had three dogs would sure get tired."

"Exactly. The sheer mathematics of it . . . hmmm, I seem to have lost my train of thought."

"Railroad tracks?"

"What?"

"You were talking about trains and trains always leave tracks."

I glared at the runt. "We were not talking about trains. I said I had lost my train of thought."

"You mean you lost track of what you were saying?"

"Yes, that's another way of putting it. I suppose."

"That's what I said."

"That is NOT what you said."

"I'll be derned. What did I say?"

"I don't know what you said! I've lost my track of trainless thought and . . . shut up, Drover, and let me think." It took me a minute to unscramble my brains. "Oh yes, we were discussing your former leg. You had just lost it to a vacuum sweeper."

"Oh yeah, good old leg. I'll sure miss that limp. We've been together all these years."

"Like losing an old friend, I suppose."

"Yeah, it's kind of sad. I even had a name for it. I called it George."

"You called your limp George?"

"Yeah, I named it after Abraham Lincoln."

"He was a great American."

"Yeah. He was the best limp I ever had."

At that very moment my gaze fell upon a strange object beneath the bed. I narrowed my eyes and studied it. It appeared to be a cup, a coffee cup. Closer inspection revealed that it was a coffee cup with Ace Reid cartoons printed on the sides.

"Drover, at some point in this conversation, we were talking about blood from your severed leg. I asked if you could see a cup, and what did you say?"

"Let's see here. I don't remember."

"You said yes. Now, can you show me that cup of blood?"

"Oh, it wasn't a cup of blood. It was just a cup. See, there it is over there, and it's an Ace Reid cup."

I gave him a withering glare. "Count your legs, Drover, and you'll find that all four of them are still attached."

"One. Two. Three. Four. Oh my gosh, Hank, I've got my leg back, and my limp too! Thanks, Hank, I don't know how you did it, but I sure am grateful."

I stared at the little mutt. He was so happy. I didn't have the heart to tell him that he might be insane. Oh well. I didn't have time to think about it anyway, because at that very moment a face appeared between the floor and the bed.

It was upside-down. The face, that is. It suddenly appeared out of thinned air and it was upside-down and the sight of it sent a shock out to the end of my tail.

My ears shot up. My eyes popped open. The hair on my back went to Automatic Lift-Up and a ferocious growl began to form in the dark deepness of my throat.

Drover noticed all of this. "Is something wrong?"

"Drover, I don't want to alarm you, but a disembodied face has just appeared to our left. At this very moment, it's looking under the bed."

"Oh my gosh, that's where we are."

"That's correct. I'm afraid we're trapped."

"Oh my leg!"

"Wait, hold it, halt. Cancel everything. It's Slim. What a relief."

"Boy, what a relief."

"I just said that."

"Thanks, so did you."

"What?"

I didn't have time to make sense of Drover's

nonsense, because at that very moment he spoke. Slim spoke, that is. I don't know what Drover did, nor did I care. That last five-minute conversation with him had almost destroyed my mind.

Anyway, Slim was standing beside the bed and had bent himself into a U-shape, so that all we could see of him were his bare feet and his face. The rest of him was invisible. It was an odd sight, to say the least, and a lot of dogs would have been alarmed. Not me. I saw right away . . .

Okay, I was alarmed for just a second or two, not for long. It's hard to fool a true Head of Ranch Security.

"Hi, puppies. What you doing under my bed?"

I held my head at a proud angle and gave him Graveyard Glares. We were under the bed to escape an infantile maniac and his runaway vacuum sweeper. Thank you and good-bye.

"Don't you want to come out?"

No. He'd had his chance to enjoy our company in a mature adult manner, but he had chosen to goof off and play silly, childish games. My dignity had suffered a terrible blow, and it would take days or weeks for me to get over it.

And I had no intention of coming out—ever. He would just have to finish his life without a loyal dog.

Too bad for him.

Miss Viola Comes to Visit Me

I had made up my mind to never leave the underside of the bed, and to let Slim suffer the consequences of his foolish behavior. But suddenly he was gone and the siege was over. My guess was that he glanced at a clock, because I heard him say, "For Pete's sake, she'll be here in ten minutes!"

I shot a glance at Drover. He was still shivering.

"I think maybe it's safe to leave our drunker, Bover."

"No thanks, I never touch the stuff."

"What?"

"I said . . . I don't know what I said. When I get scared, I'll say almost anything."

"Yes, I noticed. I said—and please listen this time—I said, I think it's safe to leave our bunker."

"Oh good. What's a bunker?"

"A bunker is a bunker."

"Oh, then maybe it's safe to leave."

"Exactly my point. And I'm going to let you leave first. It's a small promotion, and it shows that I have confidence in your ability to perform a task."

"That's weird."

"What?"

"I said, 'Oh boy, a promotion.' I just hope I can do it."

"You can do it, son. Just crawl out from under the bed."

"I thought it was a drunker."

"Hush, Drover. Just do as you're told for once in your life and let me give the orders. I have my reasons for sending you out first."

"Yeah, that's what bothers me. What if I run into the Vampire Vacuum?"

"The rest of us will be right here, backing you up. Now go."

"Oh drat."

He stuck his nose out from under the bed. He rolled his eyes to the left and to the right. "It looks clear. Slim's in the living room, throwing junk into the closet."

"Great. Nice work, soldier. Let's move out."

I wiggled myself out from under the bed and shook the lint off my coat. Sure enough, the coats was clear. Coast, that is. I made my way past the Vampire Vacuum, gave it a careful sniffing, and joined Slim in the living room.

Well, at last he had gotten serious about cleaning up his house. After goofing off and wasting valuable time, he was now grabbing entire armloads of stuff—socks, pants, towels, papers, magazines, books, plates, cups—and throwing it into the hall closet. Then he put his shoulder to the door, rammed it three times, and finally got it shut.

He paused a moment to catch his breath and brush the hair out of his eyes. "John the Baptist had it right: Live in the desert and eat grasshoppers, then nobody'll ever come to visit."

He heaved a deep sigh and ran to the vacuum sweeper. I watched this with great interest and concern, and was ready to hit Escape Speed the moment I saw a grin on his mouth. But there were no grins this time. A small miracle had occurred before my very eyes. Slim had decided to quit goofing off and to clean up the house.

He dragged the sweeper down the hall and into the living room. He plugged in the cord and started sweeping the floor—and we're talking about wild, frantic activity, fellers. He had become a sweeping demon, totally dedicated to the task of . . .

Hmmm. I noticed a small cloud of dust forming at the rear of the sweeper. I cut my eyes from the cloud to Slim, then back to the cloud. It seemed to be growing. Slim didn't notice. His gaze was frozen in a wild expression, his teeth were clenched, and he was jerking that sweeper pipe up and down, back and forth.

Something was wrong here. Why was all that dust coming out the back of the sweeper? I barked

WHHHEEEEEE

an alarm. He didn't hear, so I barked again, louder this time.

Suddenly, his eyes came into focus. His head came up. He sniffed the air and coughed. Slowly his head turned around and he saw what I had seen, and what I had tried about which to warn him. About. Which.

Phooey.

The house was filled with a huge cloud of dust.

His eyes rolled back in his head. He smacked his forehead with his hand. He jerked the plug out of the socket.

"Holy cow, I forgot the sweeper bag!"

Well, I had tried to warn him.

He stood there for a long moment, as a whole movie of expressions flashed across his face: fatigue, weariness, disgust . . . then irritation, slight anger . . . then wide-eyed, teeth-gritting anger . . . then RAGE!

You won't believe what he did. A crazy gleam flashed in his eyes. He gathered up the sweeper and all its parts, stomped straight over to the back door, and threw the whole works out into the back-yard. He closed the door with a bang, dusted his hands together, and gave me a grin.

"By grabs, next time I clean this house, I'll do it with a good old honest broom, and I'll leave them lying, cheating vacuum sweepers to who-ever wants 'em." He coughed and fanned the air, which was pretty muchly solid dust. He shook his head and stared into the fog with the look of a beaten man. "Boy, I really done it this time. I hope Viola's running late 'cause . . ."

At that very moment, we both heard the same sound, the hum of a motor in the distance, fol-lowed by the rumble of a vehicle passing over the cattle guard.

Once again, Slim's eyeballs rolled back into his head.

"Why didn't I just tell her that I ain't got any coffee? I don't know how these things happen to me."

He limped into the bathroom to do something about his appearance, which was pretty awful. Even I could see that. I mean, his hair looked like a buzzard's nest. He had lint in his beard and a layer of dust on his forehead, dust on his glasses, sweat rings on his shirt, and a hole in his jeans.

I felt sorry for the poor guy, but what could I say? He'd chosen to chase his loyal dogs around the house with a vacuum sweeper, and now he would have to pay the pauper.

I barked the alarm and ran to the door to greet our visitor.

When Drover heard a car pulling up to the front door, he started barking too. Or whatever you call that thing he does. It's not a deep manly bark, but rather a high-pitched yip-yip-yip. He came halfway down the hall, yipping his little head off.

"Hank, someone's coming! I think it's a car. Alarm, alarm! Alert, alert! Car on the place, car on the place!" At last he noticed me sitting beside the door, watching his performance. "Oh, hi Hank, I heard a car coming and thought I'd better do Alert and Alarm."

"Yes, I see."

"Are you proud of me? I was the first one to pick it up, wasn't I?"

"Drover, I hate to be the bearer of bad news."

"Oh good, 'cause I hate bad news, and I'm scared of bears."

"Nevertheless, it's my duty to inform you that your Alert and Alarm was a full two minutes late."

The smile wilted on his mouth. "Oh darn. Now I'm all upset and disappointed. I thought I'd done so well."

"I'm sorry, son, but we've had that vehicle on Earatory Radar from the very moment it pulled off the county road and entered our property."

"No fooling?"

"Yes. And I can even tell you that it's being

driven by Miss Viola. Furthermore, I can tell you that she's come to borrow a can of coffee."

He stared at me in amazement. "How'd you know all that?"

"It's all in the ears, Drover. It comes from years of practice and drill."

At that point I turned my attention to other matters. There was a knock at the door. I began to wonder why Slim didn't come out of the bathroom to let Miss Viola in. Then I heard an odd sound coming from the bathroom door—several odd sounds, actually. The first was the squeak of the door knob turning, followed by a rattling sound. This was followed by a loud whack, as though someone had . . . well, kicked the door.

None of this made sense to me, but then I heard Slim's voice. "This dadgum door! I can't get the dadgum door open. *Come in!* Viola, come on in and make yourself at home!"

Oh, so that was it. He was trapped in the bathroom. Gee, this wasn't Slim's lucky night.

The front door opened a crack and Miss Viola stuck her head in. "Slim? Yoo hoo, Slim, are you here?"

We heard his voice inside the bathroom. "Come on in, Viola. I'll be right with you."

She came in and closed the door. She was wearing a long coat with a fur collar, and some kind of furry hat on her head. My goodness, she was pretty. Her eyes were sparkling and she had a smile that seemed to light up the whole room.

I'll tell you, fellers, there's just something about a woman's presence that can change a shack into a palace.

I rushed over to greet her. So did Drover, the little stupe, even though he should have known that she hadn't come to visit him. I got there first and managed to position myself between him and Viola. Then I went into Adoring Looks and Worshipful Wags.

"Hello, Hank. I see that you managed to talk Slim into letting you in the house. Hi, Drover."

Somehow the runt managed to worm his way under my legs, and when he heard her call his name, well, I guess he decided that he actually belonged there and was welcome to stay. He wiggled past me and had the nerve to jump up on her leg.

I was shocked and embarrassed. He should have known that jumping up on guests, and especially lady guests, was crude, rude, uncouth, and socially unacceptable. I mean, jumping up on cowboys and pawing their clothes with dirty feet was okay, but doing it to a *lady*? No sir. They don't go for that kind of stuff.

He should have known better. Hadn't I taught him any manners? Apparently not, although I had tried. I was shocked and . . .

But on the other hand, she didn't shriek or kick at him or push him away, and in fact she reached down and patted his head, and it suddenly occurred to me that he was butting into my business . . . and that I, uh, needed to do something to save her from his silly displays of phony affection.

I mean, Drover hardly even knew Viola, whereas she and I had been dearest friends for a long time. If any dog was going to jump on her, it ought to be ME, not Mister Hide-Under-the-Bed.

And so it was that I followed the only course of action available to me, the one dictated by hospitality, good manners, public health, and true friendship. I vaulted over the top of Drover, stepped on his nose, and threw myself into her awaiting arms—where I, and I alone, deserved to be.

After all, she had come to visit me, right?

CHAPTER SEVEN

Slim Gets Trapped in the Bathroom

"**O**ops, sorry Drover, you can run along now."
Heh heh. His nose had come in pretty handy
as a stepping stone, to tell you the truth. I never
could have made it all the way into her loving arms
if he hadn't been there. That just goes to prove that
we all have our function and purpose in this life.

Well, I guess I had put a little more oomph into
my Adoring Leap than I had supposed. It caught
her off guard and sent her staggering backward
several steps. She tripped on Slim's boot jack and
might have gone all the way to the floor if she
hadn't bumped into the wall and caught herself.

"Here, here. Down, boys, contain yourselves."
She laughed, straightened herself up, and began
taking off her coat and hat. Then, suddenly, she

61

froze. She seemed to be staring at . . . something on the ceiling. "Am I getting cataracts? Or is this room filled with . . . dust?"

Oh. She was looking at the light bulb. Yes, the light bulb and the halo of dust particles that surrounded it.

She coughed and fanned the air and looked down at me. "Is it dusty in here? What happened?"

Well, that was a little hard to explain with wags and barks, and there wasn't time for it anyway, for at that very moment we all heard the bathroom door rattling. Miss Viola pulled a little white hanky out of her purse and covered her nose with it. Then . . .

"Slim? Is that you in there?"

"Yes ma'am, it sure is, and this is a little embarrassing."

"Is something wrong?"

"Well . . . see, I come in here to clean myself up before you got here and I forgot that the dadgum doorknob was stripped out. It'll close but then you can't get it open. Threads are stripped."

"Oh my." She tried to cover a little grin with her hanky but I saw it. "How annoying."

"Right. Well, I meant to fix it six months ago but I never got around to it."

"Oh dear." She bit down her smile and shook

her head. "And now you have company and you're locked in the bathroom."

"Yes ma'am, it sure looks that way. I may have to bust down the door."

Her eyes sprang open. "Oh don't do that. Surely there's an easier way. Can you climb out the window?"

"Dunno. Let me check." We waited for several minutes. "No, it's painted shut, won't budge."

"What about the hinge pins? Can you drive them out and take the door off the hinges?"

There was a moment of silence. "That might work, only I ain't got the tools to do it with, and there's no way you can slip me a hammer and screwdriver under the door."

"Could you do it with a table knife? Just be patient, Slim, and don't do anything drastic. I'll find a table knife and slip it under the door."

She left her coat and hat on the couch and went into the kitchen. Naturally, as her Chosen Escort, I followed. Drover tried to follow but I, uh, talked him out of it.

"Buzz off, Drover, you're not invited."

"But I think she likes me and . . ."

"She was just being polite, but then you threw yourself all over her and knocked her into the wall, and I don't think she's gotten over it yet."

"But I thought . . ."

"It wasn't the worst thing that could have happened, Drover, but it was crude and rude, and what you need to do right now is to go stand in the corner for fifteen minutes and think about Manners for Nice Dogs."

"Yeah but . . ."

"Good-bye. We'll have a test on manners later in the evening."

"Oh drat."

He left, hanging his head and looking pitiful. I couldn't feel sorry for him. At his age, there was no excuse for a dog to be totally ignorant of manners and culture and civilized forms of behavior.

And besides that, I wanted Miss Viola to myself, heh heh.

We went into the kitchen. She stood in the center of the room, the cup of her left hand holding her right elbow and the cup of her right hand holding her chin. It was a thoughtful pose.

There for a second, I couldn't imagine what she was finding in Slim's kitchen to be so thoughtful about, but then I remembered. Slim had spent so much time chasing me with the vacuum sweeper that he hadn't gotten around to cleaning it.

I sat down at her lovely little feet and assumed a thoughtful pose just like . . . well, no, it wasn't just like hers. All that chin-and-elbow stuff doesn't work for us dogs, but it was a pretty good thoughtful pose. And together, we took in the sight of Slim's kitchen.

The sink: The faucet had several drips, I noticed, and Slim had tried to patch one of them with electrician's tape. The sink itself was a nice mellow shade of brown and it was heaped with unwashed dishes. Viola leaned forward and took a closer look. I don't know what she saw, but it caused her lip to curl.

The counter: Tracking Slim's activities in the kitchen was as easy as tracking a buffalo, because he had left a complete history of his work on the counter. There were two empty bean cans, four empty Vienna sausage cans, an empty jar of peanut butter; three Saltine cracker packages, as well as a number of crumbs and cookie wrappers; and a whole assortment of drips and spots of every color you could imagine.

After pondering these mysteries, Viola noticed two pots on the stove. She leaned forward, lifted one of the lids, and peeked inside. A second later, the lid slammed down on the pot, making a crack that caused me to jump. She bolted upright and a shiver passed through her entire body, and she said, *"What is that?"* She peeked again. "Oh. Red beans, covered with white hairy mold. Yuck!"

Yes, it was shameful. Shocking. Outrageous. All at once I began to re-examine my position on Staying Inside the House on Cold Winter Nights. The woodstove was nice but maybe I needed to factor in the risk of catching some dreaded disease that might court shut my career.

It was something to ponder.

Cut short my career.

Miss Viola's shivers passed and she spent a moment rearranging her face. She even worked up a smile. "Well! We need to find a knife, don't we? Where would he keep his knives?" She spotted a drawer beside the sink and pulled it out. She bent closer and stared into it, while keeping a safe distance away, just in case something might jump out at her.

Not a bad idea, actually, considering the mouse population at that time of year. They moved inside during the winter, don't you see.

She reached inside the drawer and pulled out . . . hmm, how odd. She pulled out a small pipe wrench.

"Slim, did you know you had a Stilson wrench in your silverware drawer?"

From inside the locked bathroom, we heard him say, "Huh. I'll be derned. I've been looking for that thing for six months. Reckon you could hurry up with that knife? I've read all the wallpaper twice. Don't look too close at my kitchen. It's kind of a mess."

Miss Viola and I traded wise glances. Yes, we had noticed.

She found a kitchen knife and slipped it under the bathroom door. It took Slim about three minutes to pry out the hinge pins. Then he removed the door and was a free man at last.

It was kind of a funny scene. I mean, here was a bachelor cowboy, wearing a clean shirt and his hair slicked back and his teeth brushed and smelling of bay rum, coming out to greet his lady friend. But to tell her hello and welcome her to the house, he'd had to remove the bathroom door.

I'll bet that hasn't happened many times in history.

Oh yes, and he was barefooted and had a rag tied around his wounded ankle.

Miss Viola happened to be the one woman in a million who saw the humor in all of this. I mean, she had to be the calmest, easy-goingist, forgivingest . . .

She was one heck of a fine old ranch gal, is the point, and when she saw Slim standing there with the unhinged door in his hands, the cowlick sticking up at the back of his head, and a silly grin on his face, she laughed and said, "You know, Slim Chance, visiting your house is always an adventure."

He parked the door against the wall, ducked his head, and grinned. "The house looks pretty bad, Viola, and I'm sorry. I tried to get 'er cleaned up but . . ."

But you played Vampire Vacuum with the dogs.

". . . next time maybe you'd better give me twenty-four hours' warning. This place kindly goes to seed, and it happens so quick, it always catches me by surprise." He must have noticed that she was staring at his bare feet. "I didn't have time to put on my boots."

"And the rag?"

"Oh, that's a bandage. For my ankle."

"What happened to your ankle?"

"I was hoping you wouldn't notice."

She burst out laughing. "Wouldn't notice! Who wouldn't notice?"

"Well, you know what I mean."

She cocked her head to the side and smiled at him. "What happened?"

He rubbed the back of his neck and squinted one eye. "It sounds crazy. I stepped on a turkey neck bone and twisted my derned ankle."

Her eyes popped open and she tried to smother

her laughter, but she didn't quite get it done. Out came a big rollicking laugh. "A turkey bone! What was a turkey bone . . . oh never mind, I'm not sure I want to know anyway."

He shrugged. "It was in the middle of the living room floor, that's all I can say. I've got an idea that your friend Hank had something to do with it."

Huh? All at once I found myself out in the open and exposed, and everyone was staring at me. I, uh, whapped my tail on the floor and gave them a friendly smile that said, "I don't know anything about this, no kidding."

It must have worked, because they went on to other matters. Whew! Innocent Looks had saved me again.

CHAPTER EIGHT

We Go on Strap Dog Alert

Miss Viola clapped her hands together. "Well! I came for some coffee."

"Oh yeah, but can't you stay a while? Me and the dogs went to a lot of trouble to clean this place up. It'd be a shame for you to leave so soon. You want a peanut butter and jelly sandwich?"

"No thanks, Slim, I'd better get back down the creek."

He was disappointed, I could tell. So was I. Having Miss Viola on the place was a pretty special event.

Slim limped into the kitchen and began searching for the can of coffee. It took him a while to find it, and guess where it was: in a grocery sack on the floor beside the ice box. He'd bought it two months before and had never gotten around to putting it up on a shelf.

"You save shelf space that way," he explained to Miss Viola.

Well, she had fulfilled her mission. She put on her coat and hat, and Slim and I walked her to the door. Just before she walked out into the night air, she stopped.

"Oh, I almost forgot. On the way over here, I saw a pack of dogs crossing the road."

Slim's face became serious. "A pack of dogs?"

"Yes, four of them, and I don't think they belong to anyone on the creek. I thought you'd want to know."

"You bet I do. I've got a hundred and forty-six calves in the weaning trap, and what they don't need is a pack of stray dogs runnin' 'em through fences. We had a little incident with them dogs about two hours ago. Thanks, Viola, we'll be on the lookout for 'em."

She said good night and left. Slim watched at the window until she was gone, then he heaved a sigh and turned back to me.

"That's a mighty fine lady right there. If I had any sense, I'd ask her to go dancin' some time . . . only I can't dance. Oh well, after seeing this house, she probably won't speak to me again anyways. I don't know how it gets in such a mess." He scowled and glanced around the room. "We'd better go check them calves. I wonder where my boots ended up."

He went to the hall closet and opened the door. It burst open and all the things he'd stuffed in there came spilling out. He muttered something under his breath and picked through the rubble until he found two boots that matched. He pulled on the right boot and tried to pull on the left one—and we're talking about serious grunting and tugging—but his swollen ankle wouldn't fit.

He kicked the boot across the floor—in my direction, by the way, and if I'd been half a second slower, it would have hit me—and said in a growling tone of voice, "Thanks a bunch, Hank. What do I do now?"

Me? What . . . had I asked him to step on the turkey bone? Had I planted it there, just so he could . . . oh well. Part of a dog's job is to take the blame for everything that goes wrong in the world.

This was followed by another round of muttering and aimless wandering around the house, until he found a sheepskin house shoe that was floppy enough to hold his swollen ankle. Then he dug out his oilskin coat and hat, gloves and wild rag, and we were ready for business.

He called us dogs and we went out into the cold

night air. Slim limped along in his one-boot-one-slipper arrangement. I trotted beside him, a loyal dog to the end, and tried not to notice that he looked fairly ridiculous.

We reached the corrals and Slim draped his arms over the top board. I sat down beside him and together we studied the Calf Situation. We could see their dark forms in the moonlight. Some were still snatching bites of hay from the feeder, while others had bedded down nearby. They knew we were there, but our presence didn't seem to frighten them.

We watched them for ten or fifteen minutes. I was about ready to get back to some serious Stove Guarding, when suddenly and all of a sudden, the silence of night was fractured by . . .

What was that? Barking in the distance?

Slim heard it too. "That ain't a coyote's bark. That's the bark of a dog." He cocked his head and listened. "Several dogs. Viola was right. Them dogs may try to come back. The question is, what do we do about it?"

Well, that was simple enough, wasn't it? He and Drover could camp out near the cattle. That would leave me to, well, guard the stove, so to speak. That stove sure needed guarding. You never know when someone might break into the house and try to steal the, uh, stove.

It sounded like a good plan to me.

Slim pulled on his chin and chewed his lip. He was a slow thinker, but at last he spoke.

"Dogs, I know what needs to be done. I ought to drag my bedroll and shotgun down here and camp with the livestock. That's what a real cowboy hero would do. Trouble is, I ain't as heroic as I ought to be. I don't like sleeping on the hard ground and I hate being cold. That stuff's for the young bucks, which I ain't."

He grinned at me and winked one eye. "Us older

bucks have to use our heads. You see these gray hairs?" He pointed to several gray hairs in his beard. Yes, I saw them. "Well, each one of them gray hairs comes from me making a dumb mistake. Now, it just happens that I've got exactly the right number of gray hairs so that I ain't fixing to camp out on the cold hard ground. I'm gonna break with tradition and use my brain on this deal."

Hmmm. Well, that would be something new, sure enough, but I wondered what he had in mind. If it involved me sleeping on the cold hard ground, I was sorry to inform him that I had other plans for the evening.

"Let's go to the house and think this over next to the stove. My brain works better when it's warm. Come on, dogs."

Hey, that sounded more like it. Good old Slim. What a fine ranch manager he was turning out to be. Over the years, I'd had a few doubts about him, but yes, age and experience had put a sharp edge on his mind. I agreed one hundred percent with his decision not to camp out with the cattle.

He was a very wise man—not overly clean in his personal life, but a very wise man and an outstanding ranch manager.

Drover and I went streaking up to the house. Slim limped along at his own pace. We reached the front door at least two minutes before he did.

As you might expect, Drover was moaning. "Oh, I'm so cold! I'm not sure I can make it through another winter."

"Will you dry up? Just be glad we don't have to sleep outside tonight."

"We don't? Oh good. I thought we might have to camp out with the cows."

I glared at him. "They're not *cows*, Drover. They're *calves*. Cows are adult breeding females. Calves are the offspring of cows. If you're going to live on a ranch, for crying out loud, you ought to know the difference between cows and calves."

"Okay. What's the difference?"

"I just told you."

"Yeah, but I'm so cold I can't think straight. And my leg's killing me."

"Drover, you have a morbid preoccupation with your leg."

"Yeah, it's killing me."

"It's not killing you. If it were killing you, you'd be dying. You're not dying. You're moaning and complaining."

"Yeah, but that's the first step. First you moan, then you die."

"Drover, you've moaned enough in the last month to kill off a hundred dogs."

"Yeah, I'm just lucky to be alive."

"If you're so lucky, then quit moaning about it."

"I can't. I'm freezing out here."

Fortunately, Slim arrived on the porch just then and opened the door. That was good, because I had run out of things to say to Mister Moan and Groan. Make no mistake about it, that's a weird little dog. Sometimes I think . . . skip it. Thinking about Drover is a bottomless pit.

He opened the door—Slim did—and Drover and I had a little pushing and shoving match to see which one would be the first inside. Somehow Drover won, and he flopped down in my spot right in front of the stove. I had to go to Fangs and Growls to move him out. Then . . .

Ahhhh! I did a quick circle of the spot and collapsed. It felt wonderful! No dog could wish for more than to . . . snork murk the honking murgle.

Perhaps I dozed. I mean, the warmth coming off that stove just seemed to reach out and enfold me in its warm embrace, and before I knew it . . .

Slim was sure making a lot of noise. What was the deal? Didn't he know that some of us were trying to sleep? I raised up and beamed him a glare that said, "Would you please knock off the noise and quit banging around?"

Oh. He had just dragged his mattress from the bedroom and was . . .

"Move, pooch."

Move pooch? No thanks. I had won my spot in front of the stove, fair and square, and . . .

"Okay, don't move."

Would you believe that he dumped the mattress right on top of me? I was shocked, astonished, outraged, but . . . okay, okay, if he was so determined to . . . I scrambled out from under the stupid mattress and . . .

Hmmm. Had he brought that mattress for me?

Maybe so. What a nice guy. It didn't smell so great, but what the heck, it sure beat the floor. I moved my camp onto the mattress, did a little Digging and Fluffing to get it just right, and was about to . . .

"Get off my bed, you clam-brain."

Huh? Okay, maybe he'd brought the mattress for himself, and I sure didn't have any problem with that. The floor was fine with me. I staked out another spot near the stove and flopped down.

See, I happened to know that Slim was a sound sleeper and it had occurred to me that, once he was asleep, I could, shall we say, restake my claim to the mattress.

Heh, heh.

But what was he doing with a ball of string? He'd just come out of the kitchen with a ball of string. That struck me as odd. What could he possibly want with . . .

You'll never guess what he had in mind for that string. It turned out to be a whole lot worse than anything I could have dreamed.

CHAPTER NINE

Slim's Super-Duper Burglar Alarm

I went back to sleep. If Slim wanted to play with string at bedtime, that was okay with me. I had my own list of things to do, and at the top of the list was to launch myself into a long and beautiful night of . . . porkchops around the . . . snork.

Oh wonderful sleep! Oh warm and loving stove! Oh what the Sam Hill was he doing?

I tore myself from the delicious vapors of sleep and raised up. Slim was right there beside me, kneeling on the floor. He seemed to be . . . he appeared to be . . .

Huh? Tying one end of the string around my collar?

What was the deal? How could a dog sleep

with him blundering around the house and playing with his silly string? I didn't want to appear rude, but I really didn't need . . .

There was a big smile on his face. Somehow that worried me.

"There. That's your half of Slim's Super-Duper Burglar Alarm. Now I'll hook up my end."

Slim's Super-Duper . . . what? Burglar Alarm? What was this guy doing now? I mean, did he have something against a good, honest night's sleep? Hey, I'd had an exhausting day, and if he didn't mind . . .

Tying the other end to his BIG TOE?

I whapped my tail on the floor and searched his face for some hint or clue that might . . .

No. NO!

Surely he wasn't . . . I mean, he'd come up with some nutty ideas before, but surely he wasn't thinking what I thought he was thinking. But just in case he was, my answer was NO, ABSOLUTELY NOT.

No, no, and no! I refused, absolutely refused to be . . . I mean, this was crazy!

You know what he did? He picked me up off the floor, the nice warm floor, and carried me outside—against my will, in spite of my protests—he carried me outside the wonderful warm house and set me down on the porch!

THE PORCH, which happened to be frigid and frozen and as hard as bricks. And there, he revealed the sneaky plan that lay behind all of this follyrot.

"Now Hankie, I've got a real important job for you. You're going to be the main part of my high-tech burglar alarm. You stay out here on the porch and keep an eye out for them stray dogs. If they come back, you bark and tug on the string. That'll send a message to my big toe, see, and I'll come a-running with my shotgun. Is that brilliant or what?"

I stared at him in complete shock and disbelief. *That was the stupidest idea I'd ever heard in my whole life!*

And no, I would not be a part of such a harebrained, idiotic idea. I refused. I would go out on strike. I would hold my breath until I fainted. I would . . .

He had left the door open a crack. I made a dash for the house. If I could just shoot through the crack, I would vanish into the depths of the house. He would never find me.

"Hank." He blocked my path with his foot. "Be a good puppy and help old Slim in his hour of greatest need. See, if you camp out in the cold, I won't have to."

Right. He would get a good night's sleep beside the stove and I would freeze my tail off. No thanks.

"This is your big chance to be a hero instead of a dingbat."

Oh yeah, right. A hero with no tail because it froze off. A hero with no buns because they wasted away from all the shivering. No thanks, Charlie. If I had wanted to be a hero, I would have joined the fire department. No!

"It's an easy decision for you, Hank, 'cause you ain't got a choice."

There, you see? That was the kind of ranch government we lived under. No choice, no freedom for dogs, no Bill of Riots.

He went inside and shut the door behind him.

. . . no chance to appeal an unjust decision, no chance to control our own destiny. This was tyranny! This was an outrage! This was . . .

The door opened. Drover came flying out. Slim waved his fingers and said, "Nighty-night, y'all. Wake me up when we get to the good part."

Slam.

I stared at Drover. He stared at me. He was shivering. So was I. He began to moan. I listened to his moaning and whining for two whole minutes. That was enough.

"Drover, please hush."

"What did I do to deserve this? I was just minding my own business and being a good little dog, and he threw me out into the cold cruel world!"

"If I have to sleep out here, so do you."

"But it's not fair."

"Fine. It's not fair. Life is often unfair. What are you going to do about it?"

"Well, maybe we could sing. Do you know any songs about freezing to death on the porch?"

I gave that some thought. "By George, you're right, Drover. Just because life's unfair doesn't mean we don't have to take it without a grain of salt. We'll sing a protest song, how about that? I just happen to know one. It's called 'Freezing on the Porch.' Let's do it."

And with that, we bursted into song and protested the injustice of life. Here's how it went.

Freezing on the Porch

I'm so cold, I think I'm going to croak.
My ears are froze, my breath has turned
    to smoke.
My tail is like an ice cube, my feet are
    frozen stiff
And I think I've got an icicle growing on
    my lip.
Yes, we both think we've got icicles growing
    on our lips.

It's not fair that we're out on the porch.
Slim's no friend. He's left us in the lorch.
We gave him our best efforts, for loyalty
  we strove,
And we kept marauding crinimals from
  hauling off his stove.
Yes, we kept marauding crinimals from
  hauling off his stove.

I'm so mad, I'd like to throw a fit.
But I'm so cold, I doubt that I could spit.
And if my life depended on me marking
  someone's tire,
I'd have a bladder full of ice cubes and
  couldn't even fire.
We'd have bladders full of ice cubes and
  couldn't even fire.

So here we lie, like snowballs on the
  tundra.
Freezing tail, this really isn't fundra.
What hurts the most is wounded pride:
  Slim's flushed us down the drain,
But our broken hearts are frozen and
  that helps to kill the pain.
Yes, our broken hearts are frozen and
  that helps to kill the pain.

When we'd finished the song, I turned to Drover with a look of triumph. "There! Now, don't you feel better?"

"I guess so. But I'm still cold and this old leg . . ."

"Drover, I know this is going to be a hard night for you, but . . . how can I say this?"

"I don't know."

"Let me go straight to the point and speak bluntly. I don't want to hear your whining and groaning all night. Am I making myself clear?"

"You mean . . ."

"Yes. I mean hush. I mean suffer in silence. Lie down, go to sleep, and be quiet."

"Well, I'm not sure . . ."

"Now. Good night."

"Maybe it's a good night for somebody but . . ."

"Hush, halt, stop, be still, and shut up!"

He hushed. I heard him flop down on the hard cold boards of the porch. Silence at last! I curled up near the woodpile and took one last yawn. Maybe it wouldn't be such a bad night. I mean, we dogs were equipped with warm coats and were used to sleeping outside. It's just that . . . well, once a guy gets used to the idea of sleeping . . .

"Hic."

My head shot up. My ears shot up. I had just picked up a strange unidentified . . .

"Hic."

... sound in the night, and there it was again. It appeared to be coming from ...

"Hic."

I took a deep breath and let it out slowly. "Drover, by any chance, do you have the hiccups?"

"Hic. Yeah. How did you know?"

"Because I heard you. Will you be doing this all night?"

"Well, I don't hic know. It just happened all of a sudden."

"Hmmm, yes. I see the pattern now. Since I forbade you from moaning and groaning and whining about the injustice of life, now you're going to hic about it."

"Hic. Sounds reasonable to me."

"No, Drover, it sounds totally absurd, just the sort of thing you'd come up with."

"Hic. Sorry. I can't help it."

I stood up. "Fine. Hic all you want but I'm leaving. I can't sleep with you making absurd noises all night. If you need me, I'll be ..."

Oops. I had more or less forgotten about Slim's Nincompoop Burglar Alarm, and as I was walking away, I hit the end of the string. I guess the momentum of my enormous body gave it a pretty good jerk, because all at once I heard rattling and banging and footsteps coming from inside the house.

Oh boy. He wouldn't be happy about this.

The door burst open and there stood . . . yikes . . . Slim in his red long-john underwear. His hair was down in his eyes and he was holding a shotgun in his hands.

"Are they here? Did you hear the stray dogs?" He listened for a long, throbbing minute. "No, of course not."

Walking on crumpled toes, he came out onto the porch and leveled a bony finger at me. "Listen, Bozo, this alarm system don't work with you takin' a midnight stroll. Lie down and stay lied down until you hear them stray dogs. If you wake me up again, I ain't going to be my usual sweet self. Do you hear what I'm a-saying?"

Yes sir. I melted into a puddle of dog hair, right there, and didn't move another muscle. He shook a fist at me and went back into the house.

Slam!

Silence.

Hic. Hic. Hic.

What a lousy deal. I was cold, Slim was mad, Drover was hiccuping, and there was no chance that I would get any sleep. I would have to spend the whole night bonking the snorkle donkey with grasshopper pie snurd mork zzzzzzzzzzzzzzzzzz zzzzzzzzzz.

Barking dogs? It was just a dream. But how could it be a dream if I wasn't asleep? It was a strange world and strange things happened in . . .

Barking dogs?

Against my will, someone placed hydraulic jacks under my eyelids and pried them open. My eyeballs rolled around for several moments. My left ear rose, staggered around on my head, and finally snapped into Gathering Position.

Somewhere out in the night, dogs were barking!

CHAPTER TEN

The Phony Coyote Profiles

It was a very spooky sound.

No, let me rephrase that. It *wasn't* a spooky sound, I mean, not like coyotes howling or something like that. It was kind of spooky to be awakened in the deep dark of the night, but the sound itself wasn't spooky. It was the sound of dogs . . . having a blast.

Having fun. Barking and running loose and enjoying the savage delight of being . . . well, dogs, you might say.

And that was a little spooky, because on our outfit, dogs are not supposed to be barking and running loose at night and having fun. So . . . was it spooky or not?

I don't know. Let's skip it.

The point is that I heard the sound of barks dogging and came ripping out of a ... well, maybe it was a deep sleep. In spite of Drover's hiccuping and so forth, it appeared that I had managed to catch a few winks of frozen sleep, and I was now wide awake and ready to go plunging into Red Alert.

I barked. Boy howdy, did I bark!

"May I have your attention please! We are picking up dog sounds east of the house. Red Alert, Red Alert, go to Battle Stations at once!"

I waited for Drover and Slim to spring into action. They didn't. You know what they did? Drover wheezed, groaned, and hiccuped. Slim snored. That was it.

I was astonished. Okay, I would have to go into a higher order of barking, so I switched all circuits over to Massive Barking, took a huge breath of air, and got after it. Same results, only this time Slim also yelled, "Shut up, you idiot!"

Shut up, you idiot? Was he trying to be funny? Hey, I had been stuck out on the porch for the very purpose of ... didn't he realize that ...

Ah ha. It was then that I remembered the string. You had probably forgotten all about it, right? Ha, ha. Not me. See, Slim and I had designed this very sophisticated, very complicated high-tech alarm system that used a piece of ...

Do I dare reveal our secrets? I guess it wouldn't hurt, if you promise not to blab it around. Promise? Okay, we'll proceed into the deep dark secrecy of this device—which, by the way, spies all over the world would love to get their hands on.

The heart of the device was a strand of high-tech, ultra-sensitive fiber optic string. On the house end, the string had been hard-wired, as we say, into a receiving mechanism which we called a Digital Toe. The signals were activated on my end by a special Electron Scanning Guard Dog.

Pretty impressive, huh? You bet it was. We don't just blunder through our work in the Security Business. When we take on a job, we equip ourselves with the very latest in world-class hardware, software, and underwear. I've tried to tell you this, but you thought . . .

Better mush on with the story. Where were we? Oh yes, I was just about to activate the so-forth. I paused a moment to loosen up the muscles in my massive shoulders. You see, I wanted to be sure that Red Bird (that was Slim's code name for this mission) . . . I wanted to be sure that Red Bird got a good clear signal on the fiber optical . . .

Phooey. For the sake of convenience, let's just call it a "string." Once you get started using these heavy-duty technical terms, they can become a burden, don't you see.

The point is, I lunged against the string, sending a strong electrostatic signal down the . . . well, down the string. Red Bird received the message. I knew he did because I heard him screech the code word that meant "Electrostatical message received."

The code word was . . . "OW!" Which he screeched in a loud but sleepy voice. Then I waited for him to spring into . . . snoring? He was snoring again! Hey, I had gone to a lot of trouble to send him a good strong message on the . . .

Okay, if that's the way he wanted it, I would just send him another transmission, and if this one amputated his Digital Toe, that was his problem, not mine. I backed off, put some slack into the string, and hit it with a full head of steam.

This produced another "OW" from Red Bird, but it also broke the fiber optical string. I paused, cocked one ear, and listened. More snoring.

I couldn't believe this. After all the training and preparations we had . . . what a dumbbell! I mean, we had a pack of wild dogs out there in the night, and Code Name Red Bird was in there sleeping his e away! And so was Drover, the little goof-off, and all at once the success or failure of our mission fell upon my soldiers.

Shoulders, I should say, fell upon my shoulders.

A lot of your ordinary dogs would have shut 'er down right there and gone back to bed. Not me. To reach the rank of Head of Ranch Security, I had endured many disappointments and had seen many examples of sheer incontinence. I would just have to wrap this case up on my own.

I flew off the porch and went sprinting into the Awful Unknown. Twenty yards east of the house, I switched all circuits over to Master Control's Locater Program, called "Who's There?" My ears, which are very sensitive listening devices, began picking up the sounds of barking dogs. I made a course correction, veering left onto a new heading that appeared to be taking me straight toward the . . .

Holy smokes, straight toward the weaning pen!

This was looking bad, fellers, and I sure was wishing that I had backup for this deal. But I didn't. It was me against the . . . whoever it was out there. I went to Full Throttle, grabbed a higher gear, hit Afterburners, and zoomed on and onward into the spooky dark of nightness.

On the spurt of the moment, I made the decision not to bark. Barking would reveal my presence to the scoundrels, and for this mission, I just might need the element of surprise. In fact, I would need every advantage I could come up with.

Near the southwest corner of the weaning trap, I throttled back and came to a gliding stop. I peered into the darkness in front of me and saw . . . not much, actually, just the shadowy forms of the calves. They seemed restless, nervous. They were milling around and looking off toward the southeast. I followed the direction of their respective gazes and saw . . .

There he was! An unidentified stray dog. I studied his swillowet . . . sillywet . . . sihllowet . . . I studied the dark outline of his dark outline and memorized every detail. Description: big guy, long nose, sharp ears, long bushy tail. In some ways he resembled our profiles of a prowling coyote, but I wasn't so easily fooled.

See, our intelligence reports had mentioned stray dogs, not coyotes. Heh, heh. Otherwise I might have fallen for the coyote trick. Sometimes our enemies will switch profiles on us, in an attempt to confuse us and throw us off the trail of the track. A lot of dogs will fall for it, but I had seen it before.

There wasn't much these guys could throw at me that I hadn't seen before.

I peered deeper into the darkness and spotted a second dog. Description: big guy, long pointed ears, sharp nose, bushy tail. He was following the first dog. Did you notice that the description of Dog Two was almost identical to the description of Dog One? That was a pretty interesting clue. It meant that both were using the same Phony Coyote Profile. Perhaps they were too cheap to buy two Phony Profiles and had used the same one twice.

Okay, we had smoked out two of the villains. That left . . . hang on a second whilst I do some calculations.

$4 - 2 = 2$

That left two stray dogs unaccounted for.

scanned the horizon, searching for the other two villains, which would give us our total of four stray dogs. I didn't find them. Hmmm. Well, that was all right. I had plenty of time. I was in no rush. I would just hunker down and wait them out.

I hunkered down in the weeds and waited. Several minutes crawled by.

Have I ever mentioned that waiting drives me nuts? Your active minds find it . . . I absolutely hate to sit around waiting, is the point. I'd rather take a whipping.

At that point, it dawned on me what had happened. Miss Viola had miscounted. Her report had stated that she had seen "four stray dogs crossing the road," but don't forget that she'd seen them at night, in the glare of her headlights. Headlights cast shadows, right? Okay, check out these numbers:

2 dogs + 2 shadows = 4 impressions of dogs

Are you following all of this? I know it's kind of complicated, but notice that by using the Dog-Shadow equation, we have arrived at the correct answer, the very number mentioned in Blue Heron's intelligence report.

Oh, Blue Heron was Miss Viola's code name for this operation. Sorry.

Well, all the pieces of the puzzle were beginning to fall into place. We had two stray dogs on

the ranch, not four, and we had worked out the mathematics on it. Everything checked out and now it was time for me to move into Stage Two: Advance toward the scoundrels for a closer look.

I shifted into Stealthy Crouch Mode and moved eastward on silent paws that made not a . . . SNAP . . . sound. Okay, maybe I stepped on a stupid twig, but otherwise it was a flawless . . . sometimes they put out twigs and various other obstacles, in hopes that we'll step on them and betray our position, don't you see.

It was an old trick. We'd seen it dozens of times, so it was no big . . . the, uh, twig did snap and they heard it. I stopped. Froze. Eased myself down into some weeds.

Dog One spoke. "Uh. Thought I hearding snap of twig."

Dog Two answered. "Uh."

I could hardly believe my ears. Do you see what was going on here, the meaning of this intercepted conversation? Holy cats, it promised to blow this case wide open and lead the investigation into an entirely new direction.

Maybe you missed it, so let me explain. See, Buster and Muggs were not only traveling through our country in Phony Coyote Profile, but they were also using Phony Coyote Dialect! What this meant was that they had gone to a fair amount of trouble to develop disguises for this job.

I mean, I wasn't fooled by it, not for a minute, but it was slick enough to fool about ninety per-cent of the ranch dogs in the Texas Panhandle. In other words, these guys were clever. You don't often find such a high level of preparation in stray dogs. Most of the time, they're just dumb mutts from town who drift out into the country to make mis-chief and get into trouble. But these guys . . .

This was promising to be a very interesting case, and it was time for me to move into Stage Three—confront them, expose them as frauds and charle-magnes, and order them off my ranch.

CHAPTER ELEVEN

A Slight Miscalculation, Nothing Serious

Exposing these hoodlum dogs would have been easier and more fun if I'd had Slim backing me up with his shotgun, but he had botched his part of the mission and I was left all alone on life's front lines.

That's not the kind of situation we hope for, but that's where I was. And it was time for action. I took a big breath of air, rose from the weeds in which I had been crouching, and announced my presence to the mutts.

"Okay guys, the party's over. We've had you under surveillance from the moment you set foot on this ranch. We know who you are and who you pretend to be. We know why you're here and what mischief you have in mind. Get off the ranch right this minute or . . ."

Huh? They seemed to be . . . laughing, you might say. That seemed odd, but I let them laugh. I had an idea that they wouldn't be laughing for long.

Dog One was the first to speak. "Ha! Coyote always got mischief on mind and coyote make gooder mischief than whole world."

Now it was my turn to chuckle. "Listen, Buster, you can drop the phony coyote lingo. It won't sell, sorry. In the first place, the accent's wrong. In the second place, you don't sound dumb enough to be a coyote. In the third place . . ."

At that very moment the wind shifted and I caught the unmistakable musky odor of . . . that smell was really strong, and I noticed that the hair along my spinebone had more or less raised itself, almost as though . . . and I noticed for the first time that Dog One had . . . uh . . . shockingly yellow eyes and big teeth, real big . . .

HUH?

Gulk.

My mind was tumbling through this latest churn of events. I couldn't believe this had happened to me, but all the evidence was beginning to suggest that it had.

Okay, let me explain everything and get you up to speed. Remember our discussion about the Phony Coyote Profile and Phony Coyote Dialect? Well, it had been even phonier than I could have suspected in my wildest dreams, for you see, these guys had used the Ultimate Disguise: *They had disguised themselves as themselves!*

And I had fallen for it—hook, line, and sewer. You know who these guys were? Not Buster and Muggs, as you and Miss Viola had suspected all along, but Rip and Snort the coyote brothers. Pretty shocking, huh? You bet it was. And fellers, all at once I was in a world of trouble.

They were staring at me, licking their chops, waiting for . . . something. Lunch perhaps, or supper. Nothing that would do me any good.

I tossed a glance back to the house. Slim was nowhere in sight. Racing back to the house was out of the question. I knew I couldn't outrun them. I turned back to the brothers and tried to squeeze up a casual smile.

"Well! As I was saying, Snort, it's great to have you back in our neighborhood. How have you been?"

"Been hungry."

"Yeah? And how's old Rip?"

"Been hungry."

"I see. Well . . . uh . . ." Just then I noticed an

important detail. "Say, Snort, did you know you've got a porcupine quill in your nose? You know, porcupines are very interesting . . ." BAM. He clubbed me over the head. "I guess that's a sensitive subject, so . . . how's the, uh, family?"

"Everybody hungrier and hungriest." He grinned and licked his chops. "Been long time for not eat big yummy food."

"Oh, you mean rabbits and, uh, rodents and such as that, I suppose. I mean, that's what you guys eat, right?"

He shook his head. "Guys hungry for bigger something, maybe nice fat ranch dog, oh boy."

"Fat ranch dog, huh? Gee, it's a shame I'm so skinny, right? I mean, just look at these ribs showing."

"Too dark for seeing ribs, and coyote not care anyway. Ribs good for chewing."

"Yes, but . . . listen, Snort, if being hungry is your problem, how about this. We've got worlds of dog food, great stuff, no kidding, you'd love it. Crunchy. Delicious. You've tried our dog food, right? Remember how good it was?"

He shook his head. "Snort remember crunchy sawdust. Too boring for coyote."

Boring. I ran that through Data Control and began to formulate a desperate plan.

"I'm beginning to understand, Snort. See, your basic problem isn't hunger, it's boredom. Isn't that true? You're bored with your life, with the dull routine of being . . . well, of being a cannibal. You get up, crawl out of your hole, howl at the moon, go out on the prowl, hunt, eat, and go back to bed. Snort, no wonder you're bored. That's a very boring life."

They stared at me without the slightest expression on their faces.

"See, just look at you now, staring at me with bored eyes and bored faces. You don't know what to say because you're both so boring, you can't talk." They held a conference and whispered back and forth. Then Snort came over and clubbed me on the head with his paw. "Hey, what was that for?"

"Coyote brothers bored, hit dummy ranch dog on head for fun, ho ho."

"There! So you admit it, you ARE bored."

"Coyote brothers not admit for nothing."

"Okay, don't admit it, but you and I both know it's true." He clubbed me again. "Hey, what was that for?"

"Coyote not like truth coming from dummy ranch dog!"

"Oh, so that's it. You don't enjoy hearing the truth about yourselves, that you're just a couple of miserable boring flea-bitten cannibals—and even your fleas are bored. Isn't that right?"

Their yellow eyes were flaming. "Hunk talk stupider and stupidest. Better shut stupider mouth."

I paced back and forth in front of them and gave them a minute to think. Then I continued.

"Okay guys, I called this meeting because . . . well, frankly, I've been worried about you. Lately, you've looked so . . . well, lifeless. Listless. Uninspired. Bored, shall we say." I stopped pacing and faced them. "I think you've got Creeping Terminal Entropy. Let's check some symptoms. Have you ever suspected that you have only four legs?" They nodded. "And only one tail?" They nodded. "Only two ears?" They nodded. "That's pretty boring, isn't it?" They nodded.

"And have you ever felt more like you do right now than you did a while ago?" They nodded. "Well, there you are. You're in the early stages of Creeping Terminal Entropy. But I have some good news, guys. I think I can help you."

They went into another whispering session. Then Snort said, "Rip not feel so swell, want to hear cure for Creepum Termite Hoopem-Hikem. Hunk better have good cure or might end up for coyote supper, ho ho."

"Okay, guys, here's the deal." I moved closer to them, even though I could hardly stand the smell.

I dropped my voice to a whisper. "I guess you've heard the old saying, 'Music soothes the savage beast,' right?"

Snort shook his head. "Coyote plenty savage but not like beets."

"Exactly, that's my whole point. You hate beets so you must love music, right?"

They talked this over in mutters and mumbles. Then, "Coyote not give a hoot for love."

"Okay, but you *like* music, right?"

More whispers. "Coyote not like all music, only trashy coyote song. Not give a hoot for pretty foo-foo song."

"Great! I think this will work. Don't you see, Snort? If you hate beets and foo-foo music, a trashy coyote song will pull you out of this terrible Hoopem-Hikem."

They exchanged puzzled glances and shrugged. "Sound pretty crazy to Rip and Snort."

Yeah, well, it sounded pretty crazy to me too, but I could see that it was working. I plunged on into Phase Two.

"Okay, Snort, I think we're ready. You guys have the rest of the night to come up with a trashy coyote song. Then at dawn's first light, or heck, even later, you can, well, sing it."

He grinned and poked me in the chest with

his paw. "Ha! Big joke on Hunk. Guys too bored to sing. Want to hear Hunk do song."

"Me? No, now wait a minute, Snort. See, I don't have a song and . . . well, I don't do my best composing under pressure. I'm sure you can understand that." I searched their faces for . . . something. Compassion. Understanding. Sympathy. It wasn't there. "You expect me to come up with a song out of thin air?" They nodded. "That's outrageous, it's impossible, it can't be done. Sorry."

They stood up and began licking their chops.

"Oh, what the heck, I guess I could try. But I don't have a subject to sing about."

"Hunk not sing about foo-foo or love."

"Okay, now we're cooking. No songs about foo-foo or love. Got it. Tell me more, and take all the time you need, guys. I'm in no hurry. Honest."

They sat down and went into a whispering conference. When they turned back to me, Snort pointed to his nose. "Snort got pork-um-pine quill in nose."

"Yes, I noticed that right away."

"Pork-um-pine quill make big hurt on coyote nose."

"I can imagine."

"So Hunk do song about pork-um-pine, ha ha."

I searched their faces again. They were serious. "You want me to do a song about *porcupines*?" They grinned and bobbed their heads up and down. "Snort, listen. There is nothing musical or inspiring about porcupines, honest. I mean, it's just impossible to . . . I can't possibly . . ." They raised their lips into snarls. "Porcupines, huh? No problem. Give me two hours and I'll come up with something."

They shook their heads. "Give Hunk five minutes and better have good song about pork-um-pine."

Gulp. "Five minutes, huh? That's . . . not much time, Snort, and I hope you understand . . ." He bashed me over the head. "By George, I think I feel a song tugging at the shirt-tail of my heart. Hang on, guys, I'll be right back. Don't leave."

That got a big laugh.

I turned my back on them and went into deepest concentration. A song about porcupines? For Pete's sake, was there any subject on earth less inspiring or less musical than a porcupine? I couldn't think of one. Who could compose a song about a lumbering, dim-witted animal with a pincushion on his back?

ME, that's who, and I had to do it in record time.

You probably think I choked under the pressure and failed to deliver the song, that I was devoured by the cannibal brothers and the story's over. Ha! Not even close. Not only did I whip up the song in record time, but I also performed it before their very eyes. Here's how it went.

The Porcupine Blues

Now gather around, lift up your ears,
I've got a little song I want you to hear,
About a guy who's paid his dues.
This little guy's got the Porcupine Blues.

Now, little Porky has a lonesome life.
He's got no friends and he's got no wife.
He's got no socks 'cause he's got no shoes.
He's got a case of the Porcupine Blues.

If you scratched his back, tried to be his pal,
It would hurt your paw, it would make you
    howl.
It would make him sad but he just can't lose
That lonesome case of the Porcupine Blues.

So he stays apart, wears a coat of needles,
He lives on bark, grub worms, and beetles.
If you think that's great, you'd better get
    the news.
It's a lousy deal called the Porcupine Blues.

So when you think your life's a bummer,
Be glad you ain't a porcupummer.
It's a sad old trail for the feller who's
Got a permanent case of the Porcupine Blues.

CHAPTER TWELVE

Once Again, I Save the Ranch

I finished the song and bowed to the audience. "There you are, guys. You wanted a song about porcupines and by George you got it. Pretty awesome, huh?" They stared at me without expression. "Come on now, admit that it was a great song."

They shook their heads in unison. "Not great song. Coyote not give a hoot for colors."

"It wasn't about colors, Snort. The Blues is . . . well, it's a feeling, a mood, a state of mind."

"Coyote live in Texas, not give a hoot for other state, and coyote not give a hoot for dummy blue song." He lumbered over to me and poked me in the chest. "Coyote brothers boredomed again. Tired of singing. Do something else."

"Hey Snort, I'm not a recreation director. You

can't expect me to keep you guys entertained all night."

He gave me a toothy grin. "Ho ho. Then maybe we have big coyote feast in moonlight, oh boy!"

"Okay, okay. I'll try to entertain you. What do you want to do?"

Snort thought for a moment. "How 'bout have big fight? Coyote love to fight, kick and bite, tear up whole world."

"Hey, that's an idea. You and Rip could . . ." Snort shook his head. "Now wait a minute, Snort. I hope you're not thinking . . ." He grinned and nodded. "No. I refuse. Absolutely not. I've played the part of your punching bag on several occasions and it was no fun for me."

"Ho ho! Too badly for Hunk." They began creeping toward me.

"Wait, Snort, no, hey, we need to talk this thing over and . . ."

They were closing in on me and I sure thought . . . But just then, suddenly and all of a sudden, the silence was broken by . . . what was that? All three of us stopped and listened.

Loud footsteps? The snapping of brush? A voice . . . two voices . . . several voices, talking and laughing? Holy smokes, someone was coming, and before I had time to think of who or whom it might be, I found myself staring into the eyes of . . .

Okay, let's pause here a moment to . . . remember Blue Heron's intelligence report about *four stray dogs crossing the road*? Well, I had been on the lookout for those scoundrels all night and had more or less expected them to show up at . . . well, any moment. And sure enough, here they were: Buster and Muggs and their gang of town thugs.

Remember them? They were tough cookies. They loved to fight and tear things up and . . . hmmm.

They were just as shocked to find us as we were to find them. We glared at each other for a long time, then Buster broke the silence.

"Say, what is this? Who are these chumps?"

Muggs was bouncing up and down. "It's the jerk, Boss, the same jerk that was the same guy that got us shot at."

Buster grinned. "Oh yeah, the Head of Ranch Security."

"That's the guy, Boss, that's him, he's the jerk, and that's him right there."

"I got it, Muggsie, I got it. Only this time he's got two pals with him, don't he?"

Muggs was still bouncing around. "He sure does, Boss, 'cause I counted 'em myself, one-two, and the jerk makes . . ." Muggsie's eyes went blank.

"Three, Muggsie. One, two, three."

"Three. Okay, I counted four, but maybe it's three."

"It's three. The question is, what are they doing out here?"

"I don't know, Boss, but I can ask him. You want that I should ask the jerk?" He whirled around and faced me. "Hey jerk, the boss wants to know what we're doing . . . the boss wants to know how many jerks . . . I don't know what he wants to know, jerk, but you'd better tell him real quick, you hear what I'm saying? Huh? Huh?"

I pushed Muggs's nose out of my face. "Hello again, Buster. What took you so long to get here? I thought we agreed to meet at midnight."

Buster narrowed his eyes at me. "What are you talking about, numbskull? We came back to chase your cows, and that's what we're fixing to do."

"Oh. So you've decided to cancel the fight?" I turned to Rip and Snort. "I guess you were right, guys. They've chickened out. I thought we had a fight lined up, but it seems they're scared."

Buster pushed himself right into my face. "Wait a minute, pal. I don't know what you're talking about, but me and my boys ain't scared of nuthin' or nobody, understand? And who was it that said we was chicken? I'd like to meet him before he, shall we say, loses his health."

113

Muggs got a big laugh out of that. "Oh, that was good, Boss. 'Loses his health.' Har, har, har. I liked that one."

"Thanks, Muggsie. Now, speak to me, cowdog. Talk. Who said we was chicken?" I pointed to Rip and Snort, who were watching all of this with puzzled expressions. "Oh yeah? Those fleabags called us chickens? I think that's very funny."

When nobody laughed, Buster whipped his head around and glared at his boys. Suddenly they filled the air with yucks and laughs. Buster turned his crooked grin back on me.

"Me and the boys, we think it's very funny that a couple of fleabags would think that we're chicken."

"Yeah? Well, that's what they said. I heard them myself. But if I were you, Buster, I'd be careful what I called them. They're very tough guys."

His eyes widened. "Are they now? Pretty tough, huh?" He swaggered over to Rip and Snort and looked them over. "Well, they smell tough. They stink. Can you smell these mutts, Muggsie?"

"Oh sure, Boss, I smell 'em all the way over here. And they stink, too."

"Yeah? That's what I thought. And Muggsie, do they look kind of scrawny to you?"

Muggsie laughed. "Har, har. Yeah, Boss, they're about the stinkingest scrawny fleabags I ever saw."

"Me too. Hey Muggsie, when you look at these jerks, do you feel yourself being overwhelmed, as they say, by fear? I mean, do you feel yourself turning into a chicken or something?"

Muggs was bouncing up and down, pawing the air, and drooling at the mouth. "Naw, Boss, I tink I could take 'em. Just say the word, Boss, turn me loose, I'll teach me a thing or two!"

Buster grinned at me. "What can I say, cowdog? Your pals was mistaken. I think Muggsie ain't scared. If your boys want to go a round or two with Muggsie, maybe we got time. But I hope they understand that Muggsie holds the Alley Championship in town, and it might be, you know, a short fight."

Through all of this, Rip and Snort had sat like statues, watching with unblinking yellow eyes. It was hard to say if they understood what was going on or not. They didn't look scared but they didn't show any excitement either. Mainly, they looked puzzled.

Muggs had worked himself up into a regular fit. He was dancing around, throwing punches with his paws, biting the air, and flexing his muscles. "Okay, jerks, come get a piece of Muggsie 'cause here I am! You're scrawny and you stink, and so does your momma."

Rip and Snort continued to stare. They showed no sign of wanting to join the fight.

Buster winked at me. "What's the deal, cowdog? I tink your buddies just turned into poultry, so maybe you'd better try Muggsie yourself."

Gulp. This wasn't going according to plan. I mean, I had supposed that Rip and Snort . . . they were bored, remember? Couldn't wait to get into a brawl? Well, here was a dandy fight, just waiting to happen, and there they sat!

But then it happened. In the process of dancing around and duking the air with his paws, Muggsie kicked some dirt in Snort's face. That got his attention! All at once his eyes flashed fire and he leaped to his feet.

"Dummy Mugg-dog not kick dirt in Snort face!"

And then Muggs made his second mistake. He kicked dirt in Rip's face, and that did it. In the blink of an eye, those guys went from being statues to a couple of buzzsaws. Muggs never knew what hit him. Before he could throw a punch, he was on the ground, pinned, and carpeted with coyotes.

I turned to Buster. "Well, you were right, Buster. That was a pretty short fight."

He was stunned. "Shat up. No two dogs ever whipped Muggsie. Who are those guys?"

"Oh, just a couple of scrawny fleabag coyotes

from the ranch. They're not our toughest coyotes, but I guess they'll do."

"Coyotes! Why you . . . I wondered why they had yellow eyes, and now I know. You tink you're pretty smart, don't you, cowdog?"

"Yep, and I guess you're next, Buster. Go for it."

He cut his eyes from side to side. "Hey, boys, get em, jump 'em! We've got 'em outnumbered." The other two thugs were already backing away. "Why you yellow-bellied, chicken-livered . . ." Buster started backing away. Rip and Snort climbed off of Muggsie, the former champion, and advanced toward Buster, who said, "Wait a minute. Back off. Hey, I know judo, I know karate, I'm a very dangerous . . . you'll pay for this, cowdog!"

And with that, he was gone, Muggs was gone, the other two were gone. I heard them crashing through the weeds and bushes, with Rip and Snort right on their tails. Then . . . silence.

Well! I had cleaned up another mess, solved another difficult case, saved the cattle from being stampeded, and brought the ranch through another dangerous night. I had single-handedly whipped two head of ferocious cannibals and four head of town dogs, and hadn't even gotten a scratch.

Not a bad evening's work, huh?

I made my way back to the porch, found a comfortable spot near the woodpile, and caught a few winks of sleep before daylight, when Guess-Who finally dragged himself out of bed. He wandered out on the porch and said, "What the heck's this piece of string doing on my toe? Oh yeah, my burglar alarm. I guess it broke." He looked down at me and yawned. "Did I miss something, pooch?"

Did he miss . . . oh brother! What can you say?

But it turned out all right. Slim hiked down to the weaning trap and spent several minutes studying tracks and signs. He found enough dog and coyote tracks to figure out that I had saved the ranch from a huge catastrophe, for which I received the ranch's Highest Award for Bravery—two pats on the head, one "Good Dog," and half a piece of burnt toast.

But you know what else he did? He called up Miss Viola and told her the story and then . . . you won't believe this part . . . he invited her to go dancing that very night! See, Frankie McWhorter was playing his fiddle in Higgins that night, at a big country barn dance.

But wait, before you faint, let me finish. See, Slim had forgotten about his swollen ankle and that he couldn't get his boot on, and so he had to call her back and cancel the date.

But at least he'd thought about it. For Slim, that's real progress.

Case closed.

It was pretty slick, the way I disposed of those stray dogs, don't you think? You bet it was. Some doubters might say it was just dumb luck, but don't you believe it. The whole thing was part of a very clever plan, no kidding.

See you around.

Have you read all
of Hank's adventures?